SO-AQI-828

STAR WARS

THE CLONE WARS™

3 TETHAN BATTLE ADVENTURE

Written by Sue Behrent

Grosset & Dunlap
An Imprint of Penguin Group (USA) Inc.

LucasBooks

GROSSET & DUNLAP
Published by the Penguin Group
Penguin Group (USA) Inc., 375 Hudson Street, New York, New York 10014, USA
Penguin Group (Canada), 90 Eglinton Avenue East, Suite 700, Toronto, Ontario M4P 2Y3,
Canada (a division of Pearson Penguin Canada Inc.)
Penguin Books Ltd., 80 Strand, London WC2R 0RL, England
Penguin Group Ireland, 25 St. Stephen's Green, Dublin 2, Ireland
(a division of Penguin Books Ltd.)
Penguin Group (Australia), 250 Camberwell Road, Camberwell, Victoria 3124, Australia
(a division of Pearson Australia Group Pty. Ltd.)
Penguin Books India Pvt. Ltd., 11 Community Centre, Panchsheel Park,
New Delhi—110 017, India
Penguin Group (NZ), 67 Apollo Drive, Rosedale, Auckland 0632,
New Zealand (a division of Pearson New Zealand Ltd.)
Penguin Books (South Africa) (Pty.) Ltd., 24 Sturdee Avenue,
Rosebank, Johannesburg 2196, South Africa

Penguin Books Ltd., Registered Offices:
80 Strand, London WC2R 0RL, England

This book is published in partnership with LucasBooks, a division of Lucasfilm Ltd.

Copyright © 2010 Lucasfilm Ltd. & ® or ™ where indicated. All Rights Reserved. Used Under
Authorization. This edition published in 2011 as part of the *Star Wars: The Clone Wars:
The Essential Collection* by Grosset & Dunlap, a division of Penguin Young Readers Group,
345 Hudson Street, New York, NY 10014. GROSSET & DUNLAP is a trademark of
Penguin Group (USA) Inc. Manufactured in China.

The Library of Congress has cataloged the original edition (ISBN 978-0-448-45336-1)
under the following Control Number: 2009048645

Box Set ISBN 978-0-448-45767-3   10 9 8 7 6 5 4 3 2 1

How To Use Your Decide Your Destiny Book

Follow the instructions below before reading this book.

1. Go to: www.starwars.com/decideyourdestiny.

2. Click "Begin" to launch the book selection screen.

3. After selecting your book, the scene selection menu will appear.

4. Start reading the story on page 4 of this book and follow the instructions at the end of each section.

5. When you make a decision that takes you online, select the correct box and enter the corresponding code word when prompted.

6. After watching the scene or completing your online activity, return to the scene selection menu and continue your story.

Now turn the page and begin your adventure!

It's a bright, sunny day and you and your best friend, Peder, are running through the tangled jungles of Teth pretending General Grievous is chasing you.

"He's behind you, Peder!" you yell, laughing as Peder executes a couple of inexpert rolls along the ground to shake his pursuer.

"I've managed to lose him!" he calls back over his shoulder. "But he's wielding his four lightsabers inches from your skull and is ready to slice through it."

You let out a playful shriek as the imaginary Grievous lops your head from your shoulders and you collapse, screaming in pretend agony.

As you lie there getting your breath back and looking up into the sky, you think you see a flash of silver. You rub your eyes and look again. You did see something; it looks like a ship!

"Peder!" you call, jumping to your feet. "Peder, did you see that?"

Seventy feet away, Peder is staring up at the sky; yes, he saw it.

"Did that look like—" but before you can finish your sentence, a small fleet of gunships flies directly overhead.

"Republic ships!" says Peder excitedly. "And they look like they're heading toward the mesa and the B'omarr monk monastery!"

KA-BOOOOOM! A huge explosion rips through the

air and you and Peder hit the ground, even though you're well out of the range of danger.

"Let's go have a look," says Peder, getting to his feet and dusting dirt and leaves from his tunic. "This isn't a pretend battle, it's the real thing! They're firing laser cannons! The gunships must've landed at the base of the cliff. Come on, we have to go and see!"

Of course you want to go and watch the Jedi battle the Separatists (for who else could they be fighting?) but you could both be killed. Is that a risk you're willing to take?

"There must be a safer way to see what's going on without running into the thick of a battle," you say thoughtfully.

"Well, if you're not interested," says Peder, giving you a withering look, "I'll go alone." And with that he's off, sprinting through the trees in the direction of the towering mesa.

If you follow Peder into the thick of the action, turn to page 47.

If you take a safer route, turn to page 72.

. . . and you turn to see Ventress standing over the body of the dead trooper.

"That trooper displayed more courage than you'll ever be capable of!" you holler angrily.

Ventress slowly turns to see you standing in the doorway.

"Don't mourn a machine, worm," she replies, flinging out an arm and Force-pulling you toward her. "You have a lot of spirit, youngling. But it will not save you!"

And you hear the hum of her lightsaber as the world explodes in hot, red waves.

THE END

Upon closer inspection, you see that the speeder bike is too badly damaged to bother taking. You decide you'd be better off finding somewhere to hide.

You take the stairs down three more flights and hear voices in the distance, echoing around the empty halls, making it difficult to tell where they're coming from.

Careful to stay in the shadows, you eventually find the source; it's the woman from the quadrangle and she's fighting . . .

Obi-Wan Kenobi! His blue lightsaber flashing, he blocks the woman's forceful blows and yells out, "You're going to have to do better than that, my darling Ventress!"

So that's the famed Ventress, you think, *I was very lucky to get away from her alive!*

Ventress, letting out a howl of anger, leaps at Kenobi, narrowly missing his head and knocking his lightsaber out of his hand.

"Well, now I'm impressed," says Kenobi calmly.

"Now you die!" spits Ventress as she raises her lightsabers to shoulder height to deal the fatal blow.

Turn to page 106.

By the time you make your way outside, it's getting dark. While Obi-Wan arranges transport back to the Jedi cruiser, you watch in dismay as the clone troopers carry their wounded and dead to a designated area to await collection.

"We give the troopers a proper burial," says Kenobi gently, sensing your distress. "I know it's not easy for you to imagine, but the loss of clone troopers' lives is nothing compared to the urgent need to destroy the Separatists. As long as they exist, more and more of us will die."

You nod your head quite sadly and look up to see a transport hover into view.

"Ah, here's my ride," says Kenobi with a smile. "Perhaps you'd like to come with me? You've shown great courage today and I would certainly recommend to the Council that you be admitted to the academy."

You look first at Kenobi and then the mess surrounding you . . .

If you go with Obi-Wan Kenobi, turn to page 93.
If you stay on Teth, turn to page 52.

Janu Godalhi is loopier than a P'frorin gotta-worm, you think as you follow him and, from the look on Peder's face, he agrees!

Leading the way, Godalhi mumbles to himself, "Too dangerous, far too dangerous." But he quiets down as you enter the turbolifts.

When the doors *SWOOSH* open and you step out, you find yourselves in a foul-smelling corridor that stretches into the distance.

"What is that stink?" exclaims Peder, holding his nose.

"It's possible that something has made its way down here and got caught in one of my little traps," replies Godalhi, his smile faltering.

Squinting into the distance, you see an inert form lying on the ground surrounded by scorch marks, and Godalhi's eyes narrow as he sees it, too.

You hear footsteps and the hiss of a comlink in the distance.

That sounds like clone troopers . . . or maybe battle droids, you think to yourself, when you notice that the body on the ground is actually moving!

"Quick, inside this room," orders Godalhi, grabbing you by the arm and pushing you toward a shadowy antechamber off the main corridor.

"But that body, it's moving!" you say, shaking him off. "It needs help!"

If you follow Janu Godalhi's orders, click on box B on-screen and type code word FOLLOW, or turn to page 155.

If you help the wounded life form, click on box A on-screen and type code word HELP, or turn to page 192.

If you hide and see who is approaching, turn to page 146.

Master Koon! you think suddenly. *There's no safer place than by the side of a Jedi!*

Diving out of the LAAT/i, you race across the clearing to Koon, who stands steadfastly awaiting the arrival of the STAPs. To your surprise, he doesn't insist you take cover. Instead, he turns to you and lays his hand gently on your shoulder. You immediately forget about the incoming attack and are instead filled with a sense of peace.

"If you know a secret way into the monastery, please help us," he says, passing his other hand slowly in front of your face.

"I-I-I . . ." you begin hesitantly, confusing thoughts whirring around in your brain, some so fleeting, you can hardly catch hold of them . . .

If you are able to show the Jedi the secret entrance to the monastery, turn to page 56.

If you give in to the peaceful feeling that has suddenly overtaken you, turn to page 187.

Looking over the heads of the cantina denizens, you see Godalhi and the Trandoshan disappear into a backroom.

The coast is clear.

I'm not going to be treated like a baby. I can handle myself! you think indignantly, jumping off the stool and circulating around the room.

You push through the crowd and accidentally knock the arm of a Sullustan drinking with his friends.

"Watch where you're going," he growls.

"Sorry," you say quickly. "I didn't see you there."

"Are you making a joke about my height?" he roars. "I don't want to have to teach you some manners!"

The Sullustan's companions guffaw with laughter.

"I said I was sorry!" you blurt, your face reddening in anger.

"Oh, you will be!" he splutters furiously, pulling out a blaster. Suddenly you feel an excruciating pain running continuously up and down your arm!

Letting out a piercing scream, you fall to the floor. The last thing you see before you lose consciousness is Janu Godalhi's worried face hovering above you . . .

THE END

"Where are you going, young Master?" asks the Miraluka.

"To ask the cantina owner why our refreshments are taking so long," Peder replies, disguising his real motive for talking to the cantina owner.

"I wouldn't do that if I were you," laughs the Trandoshan evilly, pulling him back down into his seat. "Devaronians definitely don't like to be hurried!"

Then, without drawing a breath, your hosts begin talking about all the services that they can provide. You're wondering how to shut them up when, from across the room, you hear voices raised in anger and the *SHHHIIIIIIING* of a lightsaber igniting. Abruptly your table is kicked over and the meaty Trandoshan pulls you behind it.

"It's Pon'Dart," he grunts. "He has business with the cantina owner."

Suddenly there's an ear-splitting scream and a red hand gripping a blaster flies across the room, bouncing off the wall behind you. "ARRRRGHHH!" you and Peder shriek in unison.

"I would advise you . . ." says the Trandoshan, calmly reaching over for the disembodied hand and prying the blaster out of its grasp, ". . . to leave, now."

Turn to page 157.

Maybe I can't handle this one on my own, you think resignedly. *I don't know anything about comlinks! Perhaps the clone troopers are hardwired for that sort of thing. If I could find one that wasn't engaged in some sort of heavy combat . . .*

Suddenly you hear the troopers descending the stairs, with the Separatist droids not far behind.

Quickly, you jump on the speeder bike and, ignoring the beat-up state of it, you take off down the corridor. Unfortunately it's making quite a lot of noise and it isn't long before you have a squadron of destroyer droids on your tail.

This can't be good! you think to yourself, as you dodge around corners, nearly colliding with more droids, each one joining in the pursuit.

Alone and lost in the maze of passageways with a band of droideka gaining on you, you're on the verge of panicking when you see someone up ahead in the hallway.

Has that person got a . . . a lightsaber?

If you ride toward the figure, turn to page 110.
If you think the person may be an enemy, turn to page 156.

It's starting to get dark as you arrive and, ducking through the curtained doorway, the strangest sight meets your eyes: creatures from all over the galaxy indulging in the greatest excesses of dancing and trading in a myriad of stolen goods!

Godalhi guides you through the crowd toward the bar and spots his Trandoshan contact, giving him an acknowledging wave.

"You wait for me here," he says, plonking you down on a stool at the bar. "I won't be long. And for Pandits' sake, don't talk to anyone."

"But I want to come with you," you say. "If it wasn't for me, you wouldn't even know that the Separatists were at the B'omarr monk monastery."

"Stay here! This place is dangerous!" orders Godalhi with some finality, pointing at your seat and then disappearing into the crowd.

If you stay put and wait for Godalhi, click on box C on-screen and type code word WAIT, or turn to page 114.

If you follow Godalhi, turn to page 59.

If you take a look around the cantina, turn to page 12.

An expertly executed getaway, you think proudly. As you really tighten your grasp on the foot, it arcs up into the air and smashes down once again.

Up ahead you see that the earlier AT-TE has already begun to climb the almost vertical face of the mesa.

Maybe you can ride this hunk of junk right up to the top . . . You just hope it doesn't have to stop to pick up any passengers! You've been lucky so far . . .

All of a sudden the AT-TE hits the clearing at the base of the cliff and shudders to a halt. It looks like your luck has run out as a squadron of clone troopers begins to approach the AT-TE and, careful not to draw attention to yourself, you slide around to the outside of the AT-TE's foot so you're hidden from them.

About thirty feet away, you see an unconscious clone trooper lying on the ground. You scamper across to the broken clone and wrestle his helmet off.

"I'm sorry about this," you whisper to him as you put the helmet on.

Your vision is limited, but at least you won't be quite as noticeable.

Hustling back to the AT-TE, you jump back on to its foot as the lumbering behemoth begins its ascent . . .

Turn to page 167.

A ventilation shaft! If you can just get the cover off . . .

You rush over and, standing on tiptoes, you grab hold of the grid covering the shaft, give it a very sharp yank, and it comes away easily in your hands.

So far, so good, you think, pleased that it wasn't more securely bolted on. Flinging the cover onto the ground, you take a few paces backward and, with a running jump, you dive headfirst inside and tumble straight down its slippery surface.

Turn to page 138.

The destroyer droid, in its wheel configuration and personal shield activated, stops suddenly as if surprised to see you.

I'm dead! you scream silently, squeezing your eyes shut and knowing that this time there's no escape.

You hear the sound of whirring parts, as the droid rapidly unfolds and its huge twin blaster arms lock securely into position.

You open one eye; the droideka is retreating!

And then you see why. You're so close to it that you're positioned harmlessly between its two twin blasters. Because of its limited range of movement, the droideka needs to back up in order to get you in its firing line!

I never thought I'd be running toward a Separatist weapon in order to avoid being killed! you think to yourself. The cruel irony is certainly not lost on you.

As you rush toward the droideka, it skids back.

But you know another droid could come along at any minute. You need to get out of here!

You see a flight of stairs in the corner of the room and attempt the most foolhardy maneuver yet. Flapping your arms and letting out a howl like a gundark, you corral the droideka over to the foot of the stairs, like you're rounding up nerfs in a field.

As the destroyer droid hits the bottom step and bounces forward, you sidestep it and, taking the stairs two at a time, you sprint up three flights, only stopping when you're far above it.

You peer down over the railing and see the impotent machine rolling backward and forward in an effort to gain enough momentum to carry it up the stairs.

You ridiculous hunk of junk! you think smugly, dropping a haywire grenade down on it.

You're just stepping into the turbolift in the corner, when you hear the droideka blow.

The doors shut and you push the down button, but it's hot to the touch and you see that the whole control panel is flickering randomly.

Uh-oh, the turbolift is malfunctioning! Wrapping your hand in your tunic, you begin pounding on the up control, but it's not working.

Blast! I'm in free-fall! you think to yourself, unaware of how many levels the B'omarr monk monastery has in total.

Suddenly, the turbolift gives a tremendous jolt and the doors slide open easily.

You're facing a stone wall, but when you look down you can see the top of the lift shaft doorway—you're stuck between levels!

Lying down on the floor, you roll out of the gap and hit the ground with a painful thump. Getting to your feet, you find yourself in a very long corridor . . .

Turn to page 103.

The AT-TE's body looms up over the side of the cliff and you leap off, hitting the ground and rolling away from the two huge front legs.

Rejoicing in the fact that your head hasn't yet been blown off, you take in the scene: You're surrounded by the remnants of a major battle. STAP fighters, battle droids, destroyer droids, and clone troopers alike, all mangled and mashed together like so much scrap metal.

And looming up behind all this terrible carnage, the great B'omarr monk monastery!

Through its massive open gates, you see the crisscross of laser fire and hear the screams and chaos of dead or dying clone troopers.

You race to the entrance, only stopping along the way to collect a blaster and a handful of detonation devices from a fallen trooper. The blaster is pretty beaten up and you're wondering if it still works when you spy a battered spider droid wave its spindly legs in the air and let off a volley of blaster fire. Sparks fly off it as the droid whirrs and struggles, before finally winding down.

GOTCHA! you smile to yourself, pocketing the weaponry and sprinting to the gates, hoping you'll get the chance to take out a few more droids!

Turn to page 32.

Abruptly, the world before you spins sharply and you fall to your hands and knees trying to regain your balance, but it isn't helping and you slowly collapse in a heap and lose consciousness.

It's then you have a strange vision! Before you, and to your right, you see Ventress and she has Peder by the scruff of his tunic, but on the other side, to your left, you see Anakin Skywalker, his lightsaber drawn.

"Come to me, youngling," Ventress purrs. "Join the dark side and I will give your friend his freedom . . ."

"Don't believe her!" shouts Anakin. "She's a liar, she will not let Peder go! Come to me and I will battle Ventress and save both your lives!"

"He can't help you, Tethan youngling," she spits angrily, drawing her own lightsaber. "If you go to Skywalker, I will not hesitate to kill your friend and then you!"

You look at the strained, white face of your best friend, the vision seems all too real . . . what will you do?

If you trust Anakin Skywalker, turn to page 61.

If you can't risk Peder's life, turn to page 100.

Oblivious to the fighting going on around her, she advances on you, her cloak billowing out behind her like the wings of some terrifying flying beast. She shrugs off her hood revealing her tattooed head. You're literally frozen to the spot and your brain is numb with absolute terror!

She gives a harsh bark of laughter at the helplessness of your situation and spins her lightsabers in slow, wide arcs.

"Not going to try and run?" she spits, guessing her action with the lightsabers is in someway hypnotizing you.

You suddenly realize that she has no idea you're holding the grenade. Abruptly that realization galvanizes you into action and you throw the device as hard as you can in her direction.

BOOOOOM!

The electric current sizzles through the air and provides a much needed diversion.

You're sprinting toward the safety of the monastery door, when you feel the hot ZING of incoming blaster fire.

The droideka! You'd forgotten all about it . . .

THE END

Of course it's worth the risk! If you don't try something, you're destined to a life of slavery in the Tibanna gas mines!

With your arms still cuffed behind your back and the gag in place, you slide quietly along the floor of the transport and, locating a gap in the tarpaulin, you stick your head out to get your bearings.

The transport is parked in a busy loading bay. Trying to keep out of their sight, you haul your body up over the back of the transport and, unable to break your fall, you crash heavily to the ground. Ignoring the excruciating pain shooting up your arms, you wiggle across the ground to a stack of crates and squeeze behind them to hide.

If the mine owner looks in the back of the transport, you're dead!

But from your hiding place, you see him jump back into the transport and drive off without checking, and you breathe a sigh of relief!

"My, my. What have we here?" you hear someone murmur from behind you . . .

Turn to page 132.

*But then again, how are you going to find the correct
gate when you're snaking around in the dark in a silver tube?*

You've just resigned yourself to joining the crowd in the
passageway when you hear a voice you recognize—Raan
Calrissian!

"Kid! Kid!" he calls and, standing on tiptoes, you spot
him.

"Raan!" you yell back and, by some miracle, he hears you!

"I'm coming, kid!" he says, giving you a big grin.

Calrissian pushes through the crowd and claps you on
the back.

"I saw the Separatist fleet arrive and I couldn't leave you
here alone. Who knows what you'd get up to! But we've got
to get out of here now," he says, dragging you back through
the crowd toward the gates. "Cloud City security is about to
close all the spaceports, we've got to hustle!"

Calrissian barges past the security droid and dashes down
the corridors. You eventually arrive at Gate 134 and board
Calrissian's ship, the *Jostaar Express*.

"Buckle up, kid," Raan calls over his shoulder. "And do
everything I say. You're about to have a flying lesson!"

With the ship's engines engaged, you exit the spaceport
and enter a battle!

Turn to page 48.

Petrified, you can't move, when suddenly you see the clone captain rush out into the open and beckon to you.

"Come here, Tethan!" he calls desperately. "You can't stay in that gunship, it's the first thing the STAPs will destroy! You must seek cover!"

You quickly run toward him, just as the first STAP flies into view and fires on the gunship.

Picking you up, the clone captain throws you into some bushes and dives in after you.

"I'm sorry I underestimated you," he says. "If you want to help us, perhaps you can find a way into Hutt Castle?"

Turn to page 111.

"I found a holo-log with schematics for some kind of a superweapon," you blurt. "Plus, details of shipments of crystalline vertex sent to here!"

"And how do you know that the Separatists are involved?" he inquires. "Did you see any proof of this?"

"I don't have proof," you reply. "But crystalline vertex is not easily obtained and if you're stockpiling anything like the amounts I saw, you're buying, or building, something expensive."

"Like a superweapon, eh?" says Kenobi. "Well, we'd better look for a terminal to discover more about this mystery weapon."

"It seems that the main comlines have been damaged. We will have to find the crystalline vertex ourselves," says Kenobi. "I'm sure if I were hoarding precious crystals, I'd have them stashed far away from the main entrance."

"Oh, but I-I don't agree, General," you say, astonished by your own display of audacity at questioning the mighty Obi-Wan Kenobi.

"Well, of course, you don't have to come with me," he says calling over his shoulder without breaking his stride.

If you follow Obi-Wan, turn to page 90.

If you follow your own hunch, turn to page 108.

You've been awake, thinking over what you're going to say to Obi-Wan, when he enters. "I trust you slept well?" he asks.

"I-I . . . yes, Master Kenobi," you stutter. "Thank you,"

"The Jedi path is not for me," you begin. "I'm sorry. You brought me here and offered me a great opportunity and I'm turning it down!"

"I half expected it," he says. "One does not enter Jedi training lightly," says Kenobi. "The fact that you searched your feelings and changed your mind makes me respect you more. Let us go to the hangar to organize a ship. The *Spirit of the Republic* is joining Skywalker, so you must leave quickly," he says.

You wish for a moment you were going with them to meet your hero Anakin Skywalker, but your mind is made up: You're leaving.

When you arrive at the hangar, you find the only ship that you can borrow is an old Credaan Spacer, but it's good enough to get you home.

"Thank you, Master Kenobi," you say by way of farewell.

"Thank you, youngling. If it wasn't for you, we wouldn't have learned about the Separatists' plans to build a superweapon," he says. "Don't forget to contact Janu Godalhi. He could use a good assistant like you!"

He waves and you engage the ship and exit the hangar. Then it hits you! You don't have to go back straight away, you can go anywhere!

If you visit Coruscant, turn to page 34.

If you visit Tatooine to see the great Anakin Skywalker's homeworld, click on box L on-screen and type code word TATOOINE, or turn to page 151.

If you return home and meet Godalhi, turn to page 181.

"Deal," you say unhesitatingly, dismounting.

"We've kept our side of the bargain, now it's your turn. Where can we find Janu Godalhi?" Peder asks.

"Two placesssss Janu Godalhi may be foundsssss," whispers the guard. "One issss the Raidossss New Library, where Godalhi oversseessss the hissstorical sscrollsss and holocronsss." The guard smiles at this before adding, "and the other isss the mossst dissssssreputable cantina in Raidossssss."

"And how do we find the library and the cantina?" you ask.

"Thatssss isss not my problem. I have kept my partsss of the bargain and told you wheressss you may find Janu. The howssss isss another sssspeeder bike altogether," grins the sentry, eyeing Peder's speeder.

"Forget it," chimes in Peder. "We need this speeder bike."

The sentries wave you through the gates and once inside the city walls, Peder turns to you.

"Great, now we're a speeder bike down and we still have no idea how to find Janu. What now, Oh Wise One?" he asks.

If you go in search of Raidos's New Library, turn to page 63.

If you check out the cantina in Raidos, turn to page 177.

"Er, sure, sorry," you say. "Maybe you could talk to these droids and get them to stop this conveyor belt?"

"Why should I?" it asks in a huff.

CA-CHUNK! CA-CHUNK! CA-CHUNK!

"Because we could easily fall . . . down there!" you reply.

M-2XR peers down into the bottomless void and immediately begins bleeping at the worker droids.

CA-CHUNK! CA-CHUNK! CA-CHUNK!

"What are they saying?" you ask.

"They say they aren't authorized to turn off the conveyor belt and even if they were, they wouldn't for us!"

You breathe a sigh of relief as you come to the end of the belt, but as you're about to jump off two droids grab you and try to put you in the rubbish.

CA-CHUNK! CA-CHUNK! CA-CHUNK!

"Let me go!" you yell. "I'm not trash. M-2XR, tell them!"

The droids have managed to get your legs in the trash, and, at any moment, the compactor is going to come smashing down!

If you use threats to get M-2XR's help, turn to page 109.

If you use flattery to get M-2XR to help, turn to page 98.

"Please inform the compassionate Jabba that, although I did discover a cache of crystalline vertex within a secret chamber of the B'omarr monk monastery," you say truthfully, your legs shaking beneath you, "the whole room was blown up, the contents destroyed, as a result of the fierce fighting between the Republic Army and the Separatists."

Immediately the room erupts, while Jabba himself sits quietly upon his dais, silently considering this piece of information.

After what seems like a long time, he continues.

"Shmee zawka findoo lalee twigla," he says quietly.

Murmurs of disbelief ripple throughout the crowd. "Proka lemoo faltu zextu pala mee," he finishes, looking to TC-70.

"The selfless Jabba believes you, youngling, and considers it a great pity that such a fortune has been lost. However . . ." she translates ". . . he does not intend to lose an opportunity to make money, therefore you will be transported immediately to the Tibanna Gas Mines on Cloud City, where you will be sold to a slave trader the great Jabba knows."

"B-b-but . . . I . . ." you begin uselessly before being hauled out of the audience chamber to await deportation.

THE END

As soon as you reach the entrance, you throw yourself to the ground as a destroyer droid rolls into view. You're not sure whether it has seen you, but you're not going to wait around to find out.

You land beside a destroyed battle droid and, using it as cover, you reach ever so slowly into a pocket of your tunic and feel around for one of the detonation devices.

The destroyer droid meanwhile has unfurled itself and is firing its twin blasters at the clone troopers to your right on the far side of the courtyard; the noise and smoke provide a good distraction.

Found it! Your fingers tighten around a device and you pull it out of your pocket. It's a detonator, and you'll need to stand up in order to throw it as you're too far away and it's impossible to throw accurately from a prone position.

Little by little, you roll over and sit up, never taking your eyes off the destroyer droid.

So far, so good . . . you think, the droid still very much engaged with the troopers.

Carefully, you get to your feet and activate the grenade, positioning yourself to throw it, when from behind you, you hear someone speak.

"Aren't you a little small to be a clone trooper?" it asks.

Turn to page 144.

You don't have a good feeling about accompanying a complete stranger to visit a big band of criminals.

"Thanks for the offer, Janu," you say. "But I really think I ought to be heading back to look for my friend, Peder."

"I'm afraid you can never return to the monastery, youngling," Godalhi sighs. "And it's very unlikely you'll be able to go home, either," he says sadly. "I'll have to hide you here, at the library, at least for a while."

"What do you mean?" you ask desperately.

"If the Separatists are building a superweapon able to bring down the might of the Republic Army, and I believe they are, they're not going to allow someone who may quite possibly have seen their secret plans to continue to live."

"What?! But I didn't see anything!" you say, appalled.

"But they don't know that. Did anyone see you at the monastery?" Godalhi asks. "I mean apart from clone troopers and droids?"

"Well . . . there was a woman. Tall with a shaved head and tattoos."

"Ventress!" spits Godalhi. "Count Dooku's personal assassin. Things are worse than I thought. Your whole family could be in danger if you return to your home."

You drop your head into your hands in defeat. You're a prisoner at the library—the Separatists have won again!

THE END

You quickly set the hyperspace coordinates for Coruscant and you're on your way.

As soon as you reach Coruscant, you start visiting all the places you've only dreamed of. But it's the Senate building that leaves you dumbstruck.

"Come over here, youngling," calls a security guard, eyeing your tunic. "I notice you're not from here."

"No, sir," you reply, not the least bit offended. "I'm visiting from my homeworld of Teth and I've always wanted to see the Senate building."

"Ahhh, I've been to Teth myself. Pretty planet," says the guard, smiling. "Would you like to see the Grand Convocation Chamber? I can let you peek in but you'll have to be quiet as the Senate is now in session."

You nod your head happily, hardly daring to believe your luck and following the guard to a tiny side door, you enter. In the middle of the Chamber Supreme, Chancellor Palatine is speaking from his central Podium.

"That may be so, Senator Amidala," he is saying. "But taking impulsive action against the Separatists has yet to be a successful strategy."

It's then you catch sight of Senator Padmé Amidala hovering on her repulsorpod . . . and she doesn't look happy!

Turn to page 140.

"Thank goodness you're okay!" you say, relief flooding your voice. "If anything had happened to you, I wouldn't have ever been able to forgive myself."

"Uh, yeah, something did happen to me. I've hurt my ankle, remember?" replies Peder, embarrassed by your display of affection. "Now did you hear what I said? I found the turbolift!"

You glance behind you and see that the clone troopers are already checking it out.

"Is it working?" you ask Peder quietly.

"Yeah, there's nothing wrong with it. Pretty cool, huh?" he replies, giving you a wink.

Suddenly, the clone trooper leader is by your side.

"Are you still coming?" he asks, looking at Peder meaningfully.

Turn to page 67.

Suddenly, you feel the speeder bike disappear from under you as Obi-Wan uses the Force to send you both flying into the turbolift, just as the doors swish closed behind you. The speeder smashes into them!

"That was close!" you exclaim.

"Extremely," says Obi-Wan coolly, as the lift begins its descent. "Now, please excuse me if this sounds rude, but what's a young Tethan like you doing racing speeder bikes inside a smuggler's hideout in the middle of a battle?"

"So the rumors about the B'omarr monk monastery being a smuggler's den are true?" you ask.

"Oh, most certainly!" replies Obi-Wan, keeping an eye on where the lift is heading. "Why do you ask?"

You tell Kenobi about the moon-sized superweapon you saw displayed on the comlink, along with the little you know of the crystalline vertex deliveries.

"I agree with you," says Kenobi at the end of your explanation. "This weapon is too huge to belong to smugglers, it can only be the work of the Separatists."

"And what are *we* going to do about it?" you ask.

"We are going to organize to have Hutt Castle razed to the ground!" he replies matter-of-factly.

Turn to page 184.

Once inside the turbolift, the doors shut and you push the up control button, when suddenly the whole control panel begins flickering uncontrollably. You watch helplessly as the turbolift ascends rapidly before abruptly halting again.

You push the controls to open the doors but nothing happens. Peering through a gap where the doors haven't quite closed properly, you see you're stuck between levels! Looking around you notice a small trapdoor in the roof.

Jumping up, you manage to knock the panel out of place. You grab the edge and pull yourself through the trapdoor.

"Simple!" you say before you see what is to come.

The turbolift shaft, lined with old pipes and cables, is in complete darkness except for a beam of light streaming through a pair of open doors four levels above you. The only way out is to climb up there . . .

"Fine!" you snap, giving the cable that connects the turbolift to the top of the shaft a sharp tug to make sure it's secure. You begin to shimmy upward. You're fifty feet up the cable when it suddenly jolts in your hands and, looking down, you see the turbolift rising slowly toward you . . .

Turn to page 57.

"What are you doing, youngling?" you hear Obi-Wan scream. "Those charges are ready to blow. Get out of there!"

For a second, you think you may have made the wrong decision . . .

But you've made that decision now and it's time to act on it!

I can do it! you think. *I can make it to the opposite end of this hallway, double back around behind Ventress and her goons, and launch a surprise attack from the rear.*

. . . TINK 6 . . . TINK 5 . . . TINK 4 . . .

You leap over the charges laid out by the door and tear down the hallway.

One foot in front of the other, one more, almost there . . .

Suddenly you hear a sound . . . not the tink of the timer, a different sound, one of the blast engaging . . . and you realize you haven't made it . . .

THE END

"My name is Janu Godalhi. I'm a friend of Plo Koon. I need to approach to disable the security system," he warns the clone troopers.

"Approach!" calls a trooper.

You see Godalhi get to his feet, revealing his position to the clones in the corridor, and you wonder why he has chosen to trust the troopers.

"I can't believe he's going to disarm the security system," whispers Peder. "How do we even know they are who they say they are?"

"I was just thinking exactly the same thing," you reply grimly.

But as Godalhi walks past the crates you're hiding behind, you see him give you a signal—stay in position!—and you remember that as a security expert and one time constable of Teth, he's naturally suspicious.

"If you'll just give me a moment to disable the security system . . . there. All clear!" Godalhi calls to the clone troopers.

You hear the shuffle of feet and Godalhi, reverting to his confused old man persona (which you now think is an act to put off suspects), calls out: "I saw the Republican ships fly over this morning and I guessed they were on their way to the B'omarr monk monastery, so I was coming to see if I could help. But if it's all over, you've saved me a wasted journey! I don't want to tell you your business, but hadn't you better radio to your commanding officer that you've located a civilian?"

"Sir?" you hear one of the clones say, before—*PEW-PEW-PEW!*

"They've opened fire on Janu!" screams Peder, scrambling to his feet.

"Stay down!" you yell, grabbing the hem of his tunic.

All of a sudden, you hear the sound of running feet. It's Janu Godalhi!

Tackling Peder to the ground, Godalhi scoots behind the crate.

"You're all right!" cries Peder with relief.

"Of course! You didn't think I was going to disable the security system without checking those clone troopers were real, did you? I knew something was wrong when they didn't make a report to base."

"Who are they?" you ask, as the crate by you takes a hit.

"There's no time for explanations! I've activated a Cri'ardon field which should hold them off for five more minutes, but after . . ." Godalhi shrugs and takes out a blaster. "Here," he says, throwing it in your lap. "Stay in position and fire at anything. You," he points at Peder, "come with me, we need to get the turbolift working. Those faux-troopers have shot it up!"

You've never used a blaster before, but with your head down, you rest the barrel on the top of the crate and fire blindly up the corridor.

After a minute, the sweat pouring, you peek around the crate and see three clone troopers destroyed! Suddenly, Godalhi is behind you.

"Okay, youngling?" he asks.

"Clone troopers . . . trying to . . . kill us," you say in a dazed voice.

"Someone adept in the ways of the dark side has reprogrammed them," says Godalhi. You hear a sound: C-C-C-C-CLLLIIICK!

"The Cri'ardon field has been breached!" yells Godalhi, grabbing the blaster out of your frozen hand. "Peder is in the turbolift, come on!"

Godalhi runs toward the lift, not realizing you're too scared to move!

You hear the sound of running as the three clone troopers race past, unleashing blaster fire on Godalhi, who retreats into the turbolift.

From your position you can make out Peder's strained face, his mouth forming a large O shape as the lift doors shut. You're on your own!

Turn to page 70.

"I can't!" you cry out. "I can't murder you, Janu!"

"You humansss and your sssentimentality," says Rohk disgustedly. "Well, I can!"

And so saying he swings his blaster around to fire on Godalhi, who rapidly throws himself to the floor behind a stack of chests.

"For Lecaxx'ssss ssssake!" screams Rohk in frustration.

Everything is happening in slow motion as you watch the Trandoshan, his blaster trained on you, pushing his way through the chests to reach Godalhi. Suddenly you remember something: the detonation devices!

You picked up a handful when you first arrived at the B'omarr monk monastery. You quickly grab one from your tunic pocket, activate it and hold it aloft.

"Rohk!" you yell and he turns to look at you immediately, sensing something has gone wrong with his plan.

Seeing the grenade in your hand, he laughs shortly.

"You won't do it," says Rohk calmly. "If you activate that grenade, we'll all die."

"I know you wouldn't have let me live, even if I had killed Janu," you reply. "And for your information, Rohk, it already is activated . . . we're all going out together!"

THE END

"I'll never join the dark side!" you shout, leveling the blaster and letting off a volley of fire.

Ventress spins and deflects your blasts, advancing on you as you retreat, still firing.

"It's useless, worm! You will never defeat me!" she shrieks, Force-pushing your arm out to one side so you fire harmlessly straight into the treasure chamber.

A blaster bolt hits one of the chests and ricochets back out the door, striking your leg and you scream, collapsing as the blaster clatters to the floor and slides out of reach.

"The little worm has shot itself!" says Ventress with amusement as you writhe on the ground in agony.

She comes over to where you're lying and looms over you.

"I haven't been so entertained for a long, long time," she says thoughtfully, stroking her chin. "I think as a reward, I shall allow you and your friend to live."

You groan pitifully as she looks at your wound.

"You'll recover," she says. "But if we meet again, youngling, don't think I'll be so lenient."

And stepping over you, Ventress strides down the hallway, her cape billowing out behind her.

THE END

"I will never join you on the dark side!" you yell, backing away from Count Dooku.

"You have great anger inside you, youngling," says Dooku smoothly, unfazed by your outburst. "We will enhance that with our cybernetic 'rage amplification' and then you will be unstoppable."

"I won't do it!" you bellow at him, inching farther away. "I won't let you turn me into a . . . monster!"

"I'm afraid you have little choice, youngling," Dooku replies, Force-opening the door behind you. But as you make a bid for freedom, Ventress looms into view, blocking your path.

"Go and prepare my ship for departure," orders Count Dooku triumphantly. "And take our little prize along with you."

THE END

"There's no way I'm waiting to get blown up," you say, rushing to the door of the gunship and seeing that in the clearing, it's pandemonium!

The clone troopers fire upon the fleet of STAP fighters, while Jedi Plo Koon uses his lightsaber to deflect the barrage from the STAPs' cannons.

Two STAPs collide as they try to pull up out of a dive bomb maneuver and the resulting metallic shrapnel narrowly misses Master Koon.

Suddenly, you hear the *WHIZZZZZING* sound of laser cannon fire and—*BOOM!*—the gunship rocks, throwing you to the floor as the transparisteel screen shatters, shards raining down around you.

"I'm sitting here just waiting to get picked off!" you say as you think the Separatists are probably about to make a pass over the gunship.

Scrambling over to the door, you peek out and see battle droids entering the clearing—you have to get out of here now!

You drop out onto the ground and crawl under the gunship, listening for the STAPs. You pull yourself through the grass until you reach the other side.

Peering out to see if there's any sign of fighting, you drag yourself out and race for the safety of the trees. And not a moment too soon. *BOOM!*

The gunship has been hit! You're out of range of the fireball, but the force of the explosion picks you up and throws you against a tree trunk.

You lay there with the wind knocked out of you, knowing that you have to get up and hide from any more STAPs that might be on their way.

Dragging yourself up, you feel blood trickling down your face, but you're okay and you head toward the bottom of the towering plateau.

I should've stayed with Peder, you think, *but I'm on my own now!*

Turn to page 122.

I can't let him go off on his own like that, you think to yourself, *who knows what trouble he'll get himself into.*

You listen for a moment to see if you can hear him running, but you can't hear much over the roar of laser cannons and muffled yells in the distance. With your heart hammering in your chest, you run headlong into the jungle, following the route you think Peder has probably taken.

Along with the regular explosions of the laser cannons strafing the jungle, the sounds of ground battle are getting louder and louder. As you near the base of the mesa, you can see the occasional flash of blasters returning fire.

Suddenly, to the left of you, you hear heavy footsteps and something breaks cover and comes flying out at you, tackling you to the ground . . . It's Peder!

"What are you doing?" he yells. "You were going to run into the middle of a battle."

"No, I wasn't," you say angrily. "Anyway, I was only looking for you, so if I had, it would have been your fault."

Peder raises his eyebrow in that sarcastic way he does and opens his mouth to say something rude in reply, when you both realize you're not alone. You turn as one and find yourselves staring into the black, unblinking eye of a blaster aimed at you . . .

Turn to page 102.

In front of you, hundreds of Separatist fighters dive toward the free-floating pinnacle of Cloud City and you spot fireballs where they've connected with their targets.

The suddenness of the attack has left Cloud City vulnerable and even though security forces have flown out to meet the onslaught, there is little they can do against the might of the Separatist war machine.

"All power to the rear defense shields," Calrissian barks and, when you hesitate, he leans across you and does it himself.

"I haven't got time to label everything for you, kid," he says, throwing you a smile. "How about you get up in the gun turret and man the weapons. But don't start shooting until I give the signal! We don't want to draw attention to ourselves."

Calrissian, an expert pilot, puts the *Jostaar Express* through her paces, dodging fighters and avoiding defensive fire from the Cloud City super-cannons, and you breathe a sigh of relief as you finally leave hostile airspace without having to fire a shot.

"We made it!" you shout excitedly. "We can go home!"

"Sure we can, kid, but after I deliver this shipment of minerals to my client on Socorro," grins Raan. "Business before pleasure, partner."

THE END

You take a deep breath and think. *Calrissian! He helped me before, why wouldn't he help me again? I only hope he hasn't left already.*

As you sprint down the corridor back the way you came, alarms all over Cloud City activate. The sound is deafening.

You near the loading bay and see hundreds of frightened people pushing their way into a wide corridor.

That must be the way to the spaceports! you think, and looking up you see a sign: GATES 120–145.

The hallway is so packed with people desperate to board ships and flee to safety, that the crowd is barely moving.

I'll never make it to Calrissian's ship in time if I go this way. There are just too many people! If only there was a short cut . . .

You spy a ventilation shaft cover . . .

That's got to lead somewhere. All the ducts on this level must be interconnected. I ought to be able to find Gate 134.

But is that a chance you're willing to take?

If you take the ventilation shaft "short cut," click on box F on-screen and type code word SHAFT, or turn to page 17.

If you join the crowds thronging the corridor, turn to page 24.

Following the trooper, you enter a clearing about 1500 feet away from the base of the mesa, carefully positioned out of range of the Separatist laser cannons. You look around for any signs of Peder. Peering up the face of the towering cliff that overshadows this part of the jungle, you can make out the tiny figures of the clone troopers mounting their attack, aided by the monstrous AT-TEs.

"This way," calls the trooper, pointing toward the open door of one of the gunships. Inside, a clone captain sits in front of a huge screen, charting the progress of the battle.

"Sir, the Tethan I told you about," the trooper says, leaving you in the presence of his commanding officer, who swivels slowly around in his chair, sizing you up and not much liking what he sees.

"What are you doing out here blundering about in the jungle? You could've been killed," says the captain. "We haven't got time to help Tethan younglings who are crying out to be rescued."

"I didn't ask to be rescued," you say, your face reddening with anger. "I was brought here at blaster-point!"

"Of course, I apologize," says the captain, to your surprise. "It is just you're very young to be here in the middle of a covert battle operation."

"I'm not that young," you reply, slightly mollified. "I'm the same age as some of the Padawans graduating from the academy, and I suspect some of them are here today. And I have local knowledge of the area, so perhaps I can help you?"

You hear a rustle of robes behind you as the clone captain bounds to his feet and salutes.

You turn to see a tall Kel Dor standing in the doorway, a dark cape flung over his shoulders and a lightsaber strapped to his side. A Jedi!

"Well said, young Tethan," growls the new arrival, before looking over your shoulder at the clone captain. "Local knowledge can be very useful indeed."

"General Plo, I-I didn't know you had arrived . . ." stutters the captain, when a clone trooper unceremoniously barges into the gunship.

"Incoming," he yells.

Suddenly, you feel very small and insignificant as Jedi Plo Koon shouts his orders to defend the base, and the clone troopers, arming themselves with blasters, fearlessly race outside to face the enemy.

In the distance, you hear the high-pitched whine of the incoming fighters . . .

If you stay close to Plo Koon, click on box D on-screen and type code word STAYCLOSE, or turn to page 11.

If you stay put inside the gunship, turn to page 107.

If you make a run for it, turn to page 45.

If you follow the clone captain, click on box N on-screen and type code word CAPTAIN, or turn to page 25.

"Master Kenobi, thank you for all that you've done for me today and for offering to take me with you, but I can't," you say sadly. "My responsibilities are here on Teth. I've got to find out if my friend Peder is still alive and then I'll return here with a local security expert, and put systems in place that ensure the B'omarr monk monastery will never again be used as a haven for criminals and murderers."

Kenobi nods his head.

"Well said, youngling," he replies, squeezing your shoulder and suddenly smiling. "And good luck! That's a lot of responsibility for one so young, but I'm sure you can achieve all you set out to."

Obi-Wan Kenobi boards the transport and it flies off, disappearing above the clouds.

Turning around, you survey the scene; you have work to do!

THE END

"Is there anything you can't do?" you whisper, but you get no reply because Rohk and Godalhi have disappeared through the door and entered the chamber before you.

"I said is there anyth . . ." the words stick in your throat as you follow them and see before you the hundreds of chests that fill the room.

Rohk hastily uses his blaster to shoot one open and, coming to stand beside him, you see that it's bursting with a crystal substance.

"Crystsssalline vertex!" he says, astounded. "Hey kid, open another chest and sssee what'ssss in it."

He throws you a second blaster he had hidden inside his cloak and you blast open another chest.

"There's crystalline vertex in this one, too," you say, astonished.

You watch as Rohk goes from chest to chest, checking their contents; every one of them appears to be full to the brim with one of the most precious commodities in the galaxy.

"We're rich!" yells Quar Rohk with excitement. "With thisss much cyssstalline vertex we could buy out Jabba the Hutt and ssstill have enough left over to sssset up our own bloodworm farmsss."

"Stop!" says Godalhi. "We didn't come to rifle through treasure. We came to prove the Separatists are planning to build a superweapon."

"Ssso you sssay, Godalhi," replies Rohk, his voice

changing in a subtle way. "I came with you in order to get my handsss on this loot."

"You knew it was here?" asks Godalhi, shocked.

"You don't think I'd chance running into a bunch of Sssseparatistsss unlesss I was getting sssomething out of it, do you?" he scoffs. "And I don't mean the pittancess you're paying me for information, either."

"You can't take the crystalline vertex! It's more than likely Jabba the Hutt's. He'll kill you. We need to destroy it and make it look like an accident, then the Separatists won't suspect that we're on to them."

"What are you talking about, old man?" asks the Trandoshan angrily.

"Well, the way I see it," begins Godalhi, "the Separatists have plans to build a superweapon and they need financing. Jabba gives them the money they need, or rather he invests his crystalline vertex in the project, as insurance that when the war is over the Separatists treat him respectfully and fairly. Both parties are quite capable of destroying the other, once their usefulness has run out."

"Well, your usefulness has run out," says Quar Rohk evilly, suddenly raising his blaster and pointing it straight at you.

"You! Now nice and ssslowly, pick that blassster up off the floor, and dessstroy him!" he orders, brandishing his blaster.

"Me? Why should I?" you reply, your voice quavering in terror. You look at Rohk's second blaster that you put down only a moment before, when you went to pick up some treasure.

"I'm a much better shot than you kid, ssso don't try

anything ssstupid," Rohk says, clearly thinking you're going to make a dive for the weapon. "If you don't get rid of him, I will get rid of you!"

"You must do it, youngling," says Godalhi sadly. "I'm an old man, I've had my time, and yours is just beginning . . ."

If you get rid of Janu Godalhi to save your own life, click on box J on-screen and type code word GOODBYE, or go to page 71.

If you refuse, turn to page 42.

"I-I-I know a secret way into the monastery," you finally stutter, rubbing your eyes until your head clears.

"You are very strong, youngling," Koon says. "I believe you can help. You will lead a squadron of clone troopers to the secret entrance and then you must return home. Agreed?"

You hastily agree and Master Koon quickly organizes some troopers to accompany you. Every youngling on Teth knows there is meant to be a hidden turbolift in the face of the mesa, concealed under all the vines that cover its rocky face. You've never seen it, but you know it must be around here somewhere, if it really does exist that is . . .

Suddenly, up ahead, you see something or someone lying in the grass; it's Peder and he's injured!

"Peder, are you okay?" you ask as you kneel beside him.

"Yeah, I'm fine, though I think I've twisted my ankle," he says, clutching his painful foot tightly and, suddenly grinning lopsidedly, he adds proudly, "But not before I managed to find the secret turbolift!"

If you take Peder to see a medical droid, turn to page 145.

If you would like to accompany the clone troopers, click on box H on-screen and type code word CLONETROOPERS, or turn to page 35.

"Oh, what now?!!" you scream in frustration, the cable becoming hot in your hands.

"Hello?" you hear a voice call and you see a tall creature looming in the open doors above you.

"Hey, you," you scream urgently. "Push the down control. You've got to stop this turbolift!"

The creature disappears for a moment before reappearing.

"It'sss not resssponding!" he calls. "You'll have to jump onto the turbolift roof when it reachesss you and then jump off again when you get to thisss level."

"Isn't that a bit risky?" you yell.

"It's either that or get ssssquashed at the top," he calls again, a grin in his voice. "Now ready? 1, 2, 3, go!"

You fling yourself onto the top of the turbolift on the count of three and trip on some cables. You struggle to your feet and you see a seven-foot-tall Trandoshan silhouetted in the doorway.

"When I sssay—jump towardsss me. I will not let you fall," he assures you.

If you trust the Trandoshan stranger, turn to page 148.

If you get inside the lift and hope for the best, turn to page 83.

I've got to try something! And then you remember . . . the blaster!

Racing over, you grab the blaster from the top of the crate where Rohk had left it and bound out the door.

"Stop right there, Ventress!" you bellow, the blaster pointing right at her chest.

You see Rohk on his knees in front of Ventress, who has a dual lightsaber poised over her head, ready to strike.

"Is this a rescue attempt?" asks Ventress, amused.

"Put down the lightsaber!" you yell, your hands shaking.

Suddenly, Ventress Force-pushes Rohk to the end of the hallway and turns her attention on you. You fire the blaster, but she easily blocks it with her lightsaber.

"It's just you and me now," she purrs and, looking past her, you can see that Rohk must've hit his head when she pushed him, he's lying unconscious on the floor, though quite unharmed . . . for now.

"I'll give you a chance, youngling," she says thoughtfully. "You join me on the dark side or I destroy you right now."

If you give in to Ventress, turn to page 149.
If you fight, turn to page 43.
If you run, turn to page 121.

You watch as Godalhi weaves through the crowd and joins the Trandoshan. After exchanging a few words, the pair disappear through a curtained doorway on the far side of the room.

This is stupid! you think to yourself angrily. *I'm not going to be treated like a baby. I want to find out if this contact of Janu's knows about what's happening at the B'omarr monk monastery. I'm not going to be left out.*

Leaving the room, you push your way through the heaving throng until you reach the doorway and, pulling the curtain aside, you duck into an alcove where you find Godalhi and the Trandoshan, the latter with his blaster leveled at your chest . . .

"It's okay, Quar, this youngling is with me," says Godalhi, indicating he should lower his weapon, before turning to you. "I told you to stay put. This is Quar Rohk," says Godalhi. "He was confirming what I'd heard; the Separatists plan to build a superweapon and it's costing a lot."

"The Ssseparatists are contracting out work to different sssuppliers, ssso none of them have the complete planssss," says Rohk. "That way the planssss are sssafe from operatorsss who would conssssider ssselling the sssecret. The Republic would pay a lot to know what the Ssseparatists were up to."

Quar Rohk's eyes shine greedily. *I don't trust him,* you think.

"Have you heard how they are hoping to pay for this

weapon?" asks Godalhi. "This war must be a drain on the Separatist coffers."

"Private individualsss," says Rohk, "are willing to contribute. If the Ssseparatists win the war, there will be renewed trade talksss, and I've heard from the banking clan regarding immunity from prosssecution . . ."

"Jabba the Hutt . . ." hisses Godalhi, glancing at the Trandoshan, who just shrugs.

"Jabba the Hutt is a crime lord," Godalhi says. "He owns the important shipping routes in the Outer Rim, making him an ally to the Republic and the Separatists. He's ruthless and acquires his wealth by intimidation. When that doesn't work, he simply has his enemies murdered."

"If he's a criminal, why does the Republic deal with him?" you ask.

"The creature is a psychotic," explains Godalhi. "If the Republic displeases the Hutt, he will side with the Separatists against them. And Jabba the Hutt has a very long reach: You can't escape his revenge . . ."

Turn to page 95.

You wake up on the stone floor of a large storage room. You get up and look around the chamber seeing it's full of metal crates.

Someone must've moved you when you were unconscious . . .

With the door locked, there is nothing to do but await fate . . .

You don't have to wait long. Suddenly the door opens and framed in the doorway is your worst nightmare—Ventress!

"You're awake at last, youngling," she says, slinking into the room.

"H-how did I get here?" you squeak, your teeth chattering with fear.

"Using the dark side of the Force, I put you to the test," replies Ventress. "I gave you two options. How disappointed you must be that you rejected the Sith, and instead chose the way of the Jedi. You are sympathetic to the Republic cause and now you will suffer for your allegiance to your puny Jedi friends," spits Ventress.

"I have one last test for you," she purrs. "These metal crates hold a huge cache of crystalline vertex, one of the most valuable minerals in the galaxy. They are sealed, but it's possible to open them by using the control panel set into the wall by the door. There is only one way to get the crates open. If you succeed, I will let you leave and take as much treasure as you can carry," she says, smirking.

"But if you do not succeed," she continues with a sly

grin. "The floor will open up and you will tumble into the rancor pit below . . ."

"Don't think your clone trooper friends will come to your rescue. The battle still rages and they have already forgotten their little Tethan spy!"

"I'm not working for the Republic. Why are you doing this?" you ask.

"Sport . . ." Ventress replies, as she slips from the room.

Turn to page 159.

"The first thing we need to do is ask someone the way to Raidos's New Library," you say, eyeing the steady flow of humanity drifting up and down the street.

The third person you ask knows where the library is and very soon you're standing in a cavernous room, waiting for the porter to inform Janu Godalhi that he has visitors.

"Have you thought about what you're going to say?" Peder whispers.

"Me? What I'm going to say? This was all your idea!" you exclaim.

"Fine," Peder spits out, just as a door in the back wall of the room swings open and a short, round old man wanders in, quite clearly looking for someone.

Peder leads the way over and introduces you to Janu Godalhi.

"Ahhh, younglings," he says, beaming with pleasure. "What a delightful surprise. Please come with me and we can find some place to talk."

You're shown into another, much smaller room and Peder quickly tells Godalhi everything you saw in the jungle.

You study Godalhi carefully, noting how he never stops smiling. *He looks unstable*, you think to yourself, before recalling the fact that not only is he an expert on security matters, he has also assisted the Jedi on a number of covert operations.

"Mmmm, the Separatists are holed up in the B'omarr monk monastery, are they?" Godalhi says to himself. "You know, younglings, that the B'omarr monk monastery is being used by the great Hutt Clan—and numerous other smugglers?"

You and Peder shake your heads in astonishment.

"You didn't?" smiles Godalhi. "And that there is a secret tunnel running between the monastery and . . . this library?"

"What!" Peder shrieks, before hurriedly lowering his voice. "Well, let's go. What I mean, sir, is perhaps we can be of some help to the Republic."

For the first time since you've met him, you notice Godalhi's face take on a slightly cunning expression.

"The Republic would not take any of my advice during the Battle of Geonosis . . ." says Godalhi meditatively. Then, just as abruptly, his face clears and he looks like the same old, slightly eccentric Godalhi. "But that's all history now, of course, and if you young things want to help the Jedi, then yes, let us go to the B'omarr monk monastery at once."

You're just about out the door when Godalhi suddenly grabs you both tightly by your arms and hisses into your faces: "But you must obey all of my orders."

A shiver runs down your spine, but both you and Peder nod your heads in agreement and he releases his grip.

"Very good, very good," Godalhi smiles. "Shall we go then?" he adds, ushering you through the door.

If you trust Janu Godalhi, turn to page 9.

If you do not trust Janu Godalhi, turn to page 88.

Weighing your options, you decide that the droideka is highly unlikely to fire on you while its mistress (you can only assume that the evil incarnate now descending on you is working for the Separatists) is in the firing line.

I can probably disable the droideka with this grenade and still outpace that fiend, you think to yourself, realizing it may be your only chance.

Spinning around again to face the destroyer droid, you lob the grenade as far as you can at it, and fling yourself to the ground to avoid any fallout.

C-C-C-C-CRRRIIIICCCCCCCIIIK!

Electricity engulfs the destroyer droid and it sputters and sizzles, electric flashes spearing a few surrounding droids in the process. You've done it!

You get unsteadily to your feet, the electrified air sizzling around you, as you run to the doorway.

You haven't gotten very far when you feel something fly over your head and, all of a sudden, the woman is standing between you and the monastery door.

Terrified, you rapidly change direction and again the woman is there, blocking your way, smiling cruelly at the tortuous game she is playing with you.

"It's no use," she says brutally. "You can't escape!"

And in a few strides she's upon you, her long, thin fingers gripping your shoulder and tearing off your helmet.

"Ahhh, a youngling!" she says surprised. "How perfectly disgusting!"

Struggling to break free of her powerful grasp, you

feel the blaster and your remaining detonation devices bang against your leg. In your terror, you'd forgotten all about them! If only you could get hold of one of your weapons without her noticing.

"Make peace with your gods, youngling, for I, Ventress, am about to speed you to their embrace!" And so saying, she raises a lightsaber above her head to strike you down.

"Drop the weapon!" you hear a clone trooper yell.

Ventress loosens her grasp on you, as she glances over her shoulder to see how close the trooper is . . .

If you attempt to detonate a device that could possibly kill you both, turn to page 120.

If you think Ventress will retreat in the face of blaster fire, click on box G on-screen and type code word RETREAT, or turn to page 21.

If you tackle Ventress to the ground and hope the clone rescues you in time, turn to page 113.

If you shoot Ventress with the blaster you have tucked into your belt, click on box M on-screen and type code word BLASTER, or turn to page 160.

You want to go with the clone troopers, but what about Peder?

"Are you kidding?" he says, sensing your hesitation. "You have to go with these guys and find out what's going on so you can tell me all about it when you get back home!"

"Oh, if you insist," you reply happily.

As one of the troopers calls for a medical droid, another helps you move Peder to a safe spot behind a large rock.

"I only hope the medical droid can find me here!" laughs Peder, but you can all see that his pain is getting worse. The trooper gives him a sedative from his medpac and Peder falls happily into a deep sleep.

By the time you return, the other troopers have cleared the remaining vines away from the turbolift and have managed to carefully get the doors open, when suddenly you hear the sound of approaching STAP fighters.

Not again! you think, thankful that Peder is hidden away under cover. "Get in the turbolift, it's more secure than out here!" orders the trooper leader, pushing you inside to safety. Where to now?

If you take the turbolift up, turn to page 37.
If you take the turbolift down, click on box O on-screen and type code word DOWN, or turn to page 78.

"I'd rather die than join forces with you!" you shriek angrily, throwing another metal crate, which bounces harmlessly off the rancor.

"You may!" she yells, flinging some crates into the behemoth's face.

For a second, the beast falters, rubbing its great head, and that's your opportunity. Crossing the floor in four bounds, you dive for the portcullis and head up the passage to the heart of the rancor's lair.

You hear sounds of fighting and up ahead you glimpse daylight.

But, as you see, the light is not a door to freedom, rather a window seven hundred feet above the ground.

ROOOOOOOOOOOOOOOARRRRRRRR!

Ventress has slain the rancor . . . she'll be coming for you now!

You scramble onto the windowsill and peer at the bone-crushing drop. From behind, you hear the sound of Ventress's boots striding toward you. You turn and Ventress is there, gazing at you malevolently.

"You have nowhere to run, worm," she hisses. "Prepare to DIE!"

Ventress lunges at you, lightsaber raised to strike you down, when all of a sudden you're yanked backward off the windowsill.

"ARRGH!" you scream, watching the ground zooming toward you.

"That's enough of that, youngling," says Obi-Wan

Kenobi, astride an airspeeder and holding onto you. "Hold on!"

You do as he says and as Kenobi brings the airspeeder around to the window, you see Ventress standing there waving her lightsaber in fury.

"Thanks for the safe delivery, Ventress. Until next time!" Obi-Wan calls jauntily, giving her a wave and the two of you fly away to safety.

THE END

The rogue clone troopers fire on the turbolift control panel, causing it to sizzle and splutter.

"Shall we return to our mistress?" asks a trooper.

Mistress? She must've created this squadron of renegade clones! you think bitterly, tears springing to your eyes.

"Yes, after we find the other one. The one left behind . . ." replies another trooper.

You know that genetic programming has eliminated all forms of individualism from clone troopers, but you don't like that sinister tone.

Holding your breath, you listen as the troopers begin searching for you, and you soon spy the armored boot of a trooper . . . that's it, they've found you!

"Over here!" he calls to his fellows, as he bends down and drags you out from behind the crate by your ankles.

You struggle against his vicelike grip, but it's useless and after a few seconds you give up.

When the trooper releases his hold, the head trooper orders you to your feet and they surround you.

"This way," drones the head trooper, indicating the dark corridor that leads directly to the B'omarr monk monastery.

Any kind of resistance is hopeless and you begin the long march to your destiny . . .

Turn to page 79.

You bend down slowly, never taking your eyes off Janu Godalhi, and pick up the blaster. The weapon feels like the heaviest thing in the world and as you point it at Janu, he smiles sweetly and nods his head.

"You have to do this, youngling," he says softly. "I've spent my whole life trying to protect the innocent by building more and more complex security systems. But I've never had to put my life on the line to save anyone before and now here, at the end of my days, it pleases me to know that I was able to do so . . ."

Your hands begin to shake uncontrollably and tears start running down your face.

"Enough of the grand sssspeechesss, get on with it," hisses Rohk. "Dessstroy him!"

"I am not afraid, youngling," whispers Janu. "You shouldn't be, either . . ."

And squeezing your eyes tightly shut, you fire . . .

Turn to page 175.

You're watching Peder disappear into the heart of the jungle when, without warning, you hear the sound of trees crashing and a heavy, *THUNK* coming from behind you.

This can't be good, you murmur to yourself. You realize you're caught between a battle and an unknown assailant!

Abruptly, the huge form of an AT-TE walker looms above the tree line about three hundred feet away from where you're standing, and it's coming straight for you!

Hiding in a nearby bush, you watch the AT-TE approach. The ground jolts with every step and, from your hiding place, you soon spot the clone troopers advancing behind their imposing forward guard.

It looks like the Separatists have started something and the Republic means to finish it, you think to yourself, *and I intend to help them.*

The first thing you need to do is make contact with the clone troopers and offer your assistance. But will they take it or will they treat you like a stupid youngling? Perhaps you're better off doing things your own way . . .

If you help the clone troopers, turn to page 124.
If you do things your own way, turn to page 134.

"Wait," you hiss to Peder. "I think we should just trust the Miraluka. He is trying to help us, sort of, and I just want to get out of here and find Janu. What do you say?"

Peder sneaks a peek at the Miraluka and then looks back at you.

"If you say so," he replies uncertainly.

"Good, that's decided then," you say firmly, before turning your attention to the still bickering Miraluka and Trandoshan.

"Yes, hi, um . . . look . . . we are looking for someone, it is true," you begin.

Two sets of eyes swivel around to directly meet yours.

"But we only need one of you to help us and I'm . . . er . . . sorry, but it's . . . it's you," you say awkwardly, turning to the Miraluka.

"Very pleased to be of service, younglings," he says, smugly.

"Hmph! You'll regret that decision," growls the Trandoshan, getting to his feet. "The Miraluka is not trussstworthy. Thisss will end badly for you."

"Is that a threat?" you ask the Trandoshan angrily.

"No, that isss a promissse," replies the Trandoshan, stomping off.

"Allow me to introduce myself. Lippoo at your service," says the Miraluka with a bow. "Now to business, who exactly are we looking for?"

"Janu Godalhi," you reply, pleased that Lippoo is happy to help.

"Oh, easy!" says Lippoo confidently. "I know where to find him. Shall we go now?"

The three of you head out into the street, and as Peder collects the speeder bike, Lippoo tells you that at this time of day, Godalhi can usually be found at the Raidos New Library.

"It will not take long," he assures you. "I know a shortcut."

You're walking down the busy thoroughfare when Lippoo points out a very narrow alleyway on your left, more a passageway than a street.

"Down here," he says. "It's safe . . . during the day at least."

The alley is so narrow, you have to go single file: you first, Peder behind you, and Lippoo bringing up the rear.

Suddenly, behind you, you hear a dull thud and spinning around you see Peder crumpled on the ground jammed between the speeder bike and the alley wall.

"Peder!" you exclaim, bending down by your friend's side. "What happened?" you ask Lippoo, looking up questioningly.

"This happened," says Lippoo innocently, a sandbag swinging from his hands. "I hit him over the head! He'll be fine when he wakes up."

"What? W-w-w-hy?" Terrified, you back away from the Miraluka.

"Because I want the speeder bike and any money you might have," he replies calmly. "Oh, and don't bother running, this alley is a dead end."

You open your mouth to scream just as the sandbag comes crashing down on your head.

"Sweet dreams," is the last thing you hear Lippoo say.

THE END

"What makes you think that I'm on a mission here?" you ask, stalling for time. You're wary of joining forces with a Trandoshan whose services can be bought and sold. He could be a bounty hunter, for Pandits' sake!

"I don't know any other reassson why you'd risssk getting blown up by Ssseparatissst bombsss," he replies, and, as if to illustrate his point, you hear another explosion nearby. "If you don't want to tell me, that isss your busssinesss," rasps Rohk. "But we musssst get away from here."

Finding a grand staircase—you're not willing to take another turbolift—you descend two more levels until the sound of fighting becomes muffled, all the while mulling over what Rohk meant by "working together." Finally, unable to contain your curiosity, you ask him.

"Ssssimply that I'm looking for ssssomething hidden in thisss monassstery and it might be usssseful to have ssssomeone to help me move it when I find it," says Rohk mysteriously.

Against your better judgment, you're intrigued.

"How do I know that after I help you, you won't kill me?" you ask.

"Well . . ." replies Rohk, shrugging his shoulders. "You don't."

Suddenly he lunges for you, grabbing your arm. "Don't make another move!" he says, his sharp claws digging into you.

"Hey!" you yell, trying to shake him off. "Let go of me!"

"Listen to what I say or your next move could be your lasssst!"

Terrified, you look at him and realize you've underestimated this imposing Trandoshan.

"What are you going to do with me?" you ask, your knees shaking.

"I?" he replies, as he drags you back. "Nothing, but the sssecurity beamsss crisss-crosssing this hallway would have killed you."

You look down the hallway; it looks like every other one you've seen!

"What security beams?" you ask, puzzled. "I don't see anything."

"It isss because my eyessight isss far sssuperior," says Rohk, rolling his large eyes. "I'm able to sssee far into the infrared ssspectrumsss."

"Thank you," you say. "That's the second time you've saved my life."

But Rohk isn't listening. Instead, he drops to the ground and, wriggling forward on his stomach, pulls himself deftly down the corridor, looking very much like the reptilian creature that he is.

"What are you doing?" you ask with surprise.

"You've dissscovered what I've been sssearching for," he hisses. "A ssseemingly ordinary hallway with an unusual amount of sssecurity," he replies, getting to his feet and peering at a door leading off the hallway.

"Asssk yoursssself why thisss door should be so heavily guarded," he replies and feeling his way around the outside of the door he finds what he's looking for—a control panel, it's almost invisible to the naked eye. Using his claws, he rips the cover off and peeps inside. "It can only be becaussse sssomething of immenssse value isss hidden inssside."

You watch as he uses his razor-sharp claws to cut the wiring inside and the door whooshes open.

"Aha!" you hear Rohk exclaim as he disappears into the room.

Turn to page 118.

As the doors close, you see a STAP hover into view and open fire on the exposed clone troopers and you pray that they make it out alive, although you don't hold out much hope.

You push the down button and the lift descends; you don't know where you're going, you only want to get away from the awful scene you just witnessed.

After a moment, it stops and the doors slide open to reveal a deserted corridor . . .

Turn to page 103.

The walk seems interminable and you wonder if Janu Godalhi has any more surprises up his sleeve—booby traps or even a rescue attempt.

But an hour later, when you find yourself facing a matching set of turbolifts leading up to the monastery, you realize you're going to have to get yourself out of this horrid situation.

The doors *SWOOSH* open and the troopers push you inside.

"Where are we going?" you ask them for the billionth time and, like all the other times before, they ignore you.

You're getting desperate! They're going to hand you over to their "mistress," someone powerful enough to reprogram clone troopers trained since birth to be fiercely loyal to their Republic masters, and you don't imagine she's going to let you leave the B'omarr monk monastery alive.

"Okay," you say anxiously. "At least tell me why you didn't just kill me back there? Why have you brought me here to the monastery?"

Again you're met with deathly silence.

"Answer me! I command you to answer me!" you yell, fear and frustration suddenly intermingling explosively and morphing into red-hot anger.

The turbolift doors suddenly open and you step into an enormous, empty chamber. Far above you, you hear the muffled sounds of laser fire and the dull thud of explosions, but in your fury, the Separatist invasion is forgotten.

"When I give an order, I expect it to be obeyed!" you rage impotently. "Your Kaminoan training sergeants would be ashamed of you if they could see you now!"

You see a trooper cock its head as if suddenly hearing you for the first time and he immediately becomes the prime target of your wrath.

"Yes, that's right. Ashamed! Are you so badly instructed that you'd be persuaded so easily by your new mistress to forget the Republic code of decency, loyalty, and obedience to all that is right and good?!" you rant, your voice echoing off the unadorned walls and floors.

The trooper staggers slightly as if being punched in the stomach, but still appears to be listening as you frantically search your memory for fragments of history you learned at your father's knee.

From a very dark corner of the room, you hear a hiss of someone exhaling loudly.

"Enough of this!" an imperious voice calls and a tall woman enveloped in a dull gray cloak steps out of the shadows. "It was a brave effort to try to rouse these . . . these . . . robot slaves to action, but they're completely within my power."

"Your power," you say scornfully. "And who are you to say it's possible to erase years of training and battle-craft?"

"I am Ventress!" she howls. "And these drones are mine!"

Her name echoes in the chamber and you begin to feel afraid.

"Fools!" Ventress bellows, grabbing your arm and pushing you into the clone trooper. "Does this look like the human I'm looking for?"

"Orders were to find the human and bring it to you," the

trooper says.

You hear a different tone in his voice . . . But Ventress doesn't seem to notice and she turns to you again.

"I wonder if I could use you as bait!" she smiles. "Pitiful human bait to catch another human. How pathetic and predictable you are!"

Grabbing you, she pulls you close and gazes deep into your eyes. You start to feel woozy and off-balance . . .

"Soon you will be in my power and then you will call to Skywalker for help. He will not be able to refuse a request," purrs Ventress.

The sound of blaster fire jolts you out of your hypnotic state and a clone trooper pulls you out of Ventress's grasp.

"Get out!" you hear him yell as he jumps between you and Ventress.

You nod at the trooper who is about to sacrifice his life to save yours, and, hearing the sound of a lightsaber, you hurtle toward the door.

You're almost through the door when you hear a scream and a body drop heavily to the ground . . .

If you avenge the death of the trooper, turn to page 6.

If you flee, click on box G on-screen and type code word FLEE, or turn to page 21.

"It won't take a moment, I have some important information that I think the Senator would like to hear," you say angrily, though you're not stupid enough to make any moves toward her.

"You all do," says the guard wearily. "Now, if you'll just be on your way, youngling . . ."

"But this really is important!" you say, frustrated at seeing your opportunity slip away as Senator Amidala nears her transport.

"That's what you all say!" snarls the bodyguard. "If you don't leave here immediately, I'll have you arrested. Now go!"

You can't just let her leave like this without talking to her! When will you possibly have another opportunity?

"Senator!" you yell, darting forward, but the bodyguards are well trained for such eventualities and jump on you, quickly slapping a pair of security bracelets tightly around your wrists.

You struggle against them, but it's useless and as they hand you over to the Senate Guards, you wish you'd never come to Coruscant!

THE END

You've heard all about Trandoshans, how they're invariably ruthless and selfish. Why would you put your trust in one that happens to materialize inside a Separatist stronghold? That'd be madness!

Your mind made up, you quickly scramble back through the hole you climbed out of and drop down into the turbolift once again. For a moment, it seems that the lift is slowing down to stop, but then it rapidly accelerates and you begin ascending at an even faster pace.

Panic starts to take hold; have you made a mistake? Should you have taken your chances with the Trandoshan?

All the levels on the lift's control panel are lit up and you furiously begin thumping the down button, but to no effect. Suddenly, a shower of sparks flies out of it and it catches fire.

You look up through the trapdoor in the roof and see that you're nearing the top of the shaft with no chance of slowing, and you realize you've made the wrong decision . . . and it's going to cost you your life!

THE END

You shove a crate toward Ventress, sidestep out of her way, and run toward the door. But it won't budge!

"Stupid Tethan!" laughs Ventress maliciously. "Did you really think I'd leave you an escape route?"

Suddenly, the rancor gives a roar and, using its fangs, rips the gate off its hinges and steps into the chamber.

"And did you know that was going to happen?" you yell, picking up a crate and hurling it at the rancor, who swats it out of the way as if it were an insect.

Ventress, brandishing her lightsaber, jumps fearlessly toward the rancor, which gnashes its teeth, slobber flecking her face, but the rancor's arms are so long, she can't get close enough to it to land a blow.

While you hurl metal chests at the monster, Ventress dives around the chamber, trying to surprise it, but the rancor dodges her every attack, while making sure to stand between you and the exit!

"There is only one way to defeat the rancor!" Ventress shouts to you. "You distract the beast and I will attack it from behind!"

If you help Ventress defeat the rancor, turn to page 130.

If you make a run for the gate, turn to page 68.

You've barely entered his office before Godalhi launches into conversation.

"As I said before, I'm Janu Godalhi and I used to design security systems for both the Government and private enterprise. Have done it for years. Not only here on Teth, but also on Coruscant and, oh, plenty of other planets," he says, his eyes twinkling with satisfaction. "But I'm getting old now and I've returned to my first love, history. I work here, at the Raidos New Library, in the archives."

"How did you know I was coming?" you ask again.

"I didn't know it was you specifically, but I have sensors hidden all along that corridor that runs between the monastery and here, and I tracked your arrival. Then I simply programmed the turbolift to bring all persons lacking the correct security pass to this level here. And here you are!" says Godalhi. "Now, I want to know what you were doing at the monastery. You're a little too young to be a smuggler . . ."

"Smuggler?" you ask bewildered. "Of course I'm not a smuggler! My friend Peder and I were out in the jungle this morning and we saw a fleet of Republican gunships land and attack a Separatist force that has taken over the monastery and—"

"Separatists? You're sure it was Separatists?" asks Godalhi, cutting you off mid-sentence.

"Yeah, I'm sure. I saw them myself when I went up to the monastery!"

"Sorry, please do go on," says Godalhi apologetically.

"Well, that's about it. I went up to the monastery, stumbled into a faulty turbolift which spat me out in a secret passage and you know the rest," you say, shrugging your shoulders.

"Separatists, eh?" murmurs Godalhi, tapping his chin in thought. "I've heard whispers that the Separatists are planning to build something . . . a type of superweapon capable of destroying entire planets. Perhaps they're using the B'omarr monk monastery as their base of operations . . ."

"But that's insane. No weapon is capable of destroying a planet!" you chime in doubtfully, wondering if Godalhi hasn't become paranoid after many years working in the security sector.

"Oh yes, it's perfectly possible," says Godalhi, confidently. "And if they were planning something of that magnitude, a seldom-visited little backwater planet like Teth might be just the sort of place they'd hide themselves while plotting the Republic's downfall. I think you and I should go and have a word with one of my, er, associates from the, um, criminal classes."

But are you willing to consort with thieves and bounty hunters with a man you've only just met?

If you trust Janu Godalhi, turn to page 15.
If you decline Janu Godalhi's offer, turn to page 33.

You run to the door. This is your only chance, but as you reach it, Ventress stands before you, blocking your way.

"Too slow, youngling," she says, giving you a twisted smile. "Your friend is dead. Let this be a lesson to you; if you double-cross the Separatists, you will be punished!"

She glances around the chamber and back at you.

"In fact, why don't I leave you in here to think about that for a while," says Ventress mildly. "It's quite possible that someone may be along soon to let you out . . . but then it's equally possible that they won't."

And without another word, the doors slide shut and you're suddenly alone. The treasure chamber has become your tomb.

THE END

You have a terrible suspicion that coming to Raidos and asking Janu Godalhi for help was a big mistake, but you try not to let your doubts show. After all, Godalhi can probably read your face as easily as he reads the thousands of Holocrons stored within the Library.

You pass through the door and Godalhi tells you he must go along to his office to collect the passkey to the door of the secret tunnel.

"Obviously we don't let people down there and it's all locked up against intruders coming from, ahem, the other side, as it were," he says, beaming and leading the way down the corridor. "Come along, I won't be a moment."

You drop back a bit and hope Peder takes the hint to slow down so you can talk privately and, sure enough, with hand gestures and a lot of eye rolling, Peder manages to convey the fact that he feels the same way you do.

"What do you propose we do?" he murmurs under his breath.

You shrug your shoulders helplessly, furiously trying to formulate a plan that will allow you to leave without offending the old man.

Five minutes later, you're all standing in Godalhi's stark office and while he rummages around in a huge safe mumbling to himself, you and Peder signal to each other that it's about time you excused yourselves and left.

Suddenly Godalhi spins around, a blaster gripped tightly in his hand.

"I'm sorry, younglings," he says aiming the blaster at

you. "But I'm afraid I've changed my mind. I won't be able to help the Jedi after all!"

Shocked, you and Peder both slowly back away from him.

"No, please don't try and run, I will shoot you if I have to," he says, pacing up and down the office, the blaster still pointing at your chest.

"I don't want to, though. I'm not a killer; I'm just a man disillusioned with wars and politics. I want to help you younglings avoid getting involved in something that you don't understand. Good and evil are sometimes two sides of the same coin and I wish I'd known that when I was your age."

"W-What are you going to d-d-do with us?" you ask, your voice quavering and your legs shaking uncontrollably with fear.

"Well . . . I thought perhaps I'd keep you here and hold you for ransom," replies Godalhi, his eyes now glinting with the light of insanity.

"I borrowed money off your father, you see," he adds, turning to Peder. "But I'm sure he'd wipe out the debt and even give me money, if I returned his precious son to him unharmed."

You see Peder turn white and open his mouth to speak.

"Please, just let us go. We won't tell anyone about this."

"Oh, you won't change my mind," continues Godalhi, completely ignoring Peder. "I just have to think of a way to convince your father to take me seriously."

He looks over at you thoughtfully.

"Sending him something of your friend's might make his decision easier. A lock of hair, perhaps? Would you like it to be attached to the head or not?!"

THE END

But as you watch Kenobi disappear around the corner, your confidence in your own abilities falters.

What am I thinking? I'm questioning a Jedi! you admonish yourself, and chasing after him you round the corner, bumping straight into the waiting Obi-Wan Kenobi.

"Good for you!" he says, clapping you on the back. "It takes a lot of courage to admit that you may be in the wrong. We'll make a Jedi of you yet, youngling."

A JEDI?

Searching the hallways and chambers of the B'omarr monk monastery is a big undertaking, and after a couple of hours you're becoming frustrated, yet thankful you've managed to avoid further encounters with Separatist droids.

"This is going to take forever," you say with some irritation.

"Patience," says Kenobi. "Hot-headedness never achieves more than calm reflection." He closes his eyes, and with the Force, feels which way to go . . .

"This way," he says, eyes open and marching off.

You're following obediently after Kenobi when he suddenly stops outside a chamber door, very much like the seventy or so you've already checked out.

"It's here," he says matter-of-factly. "In this chamber."

After studying the access panel and finding it incomprehensible, Obi-Wan Kenobi feels for gaps around the door, which may be useful in opening it.

"And as one would expect," he says turning to you and smiling, "this security system is much more advanced than the other systems in place around the castle. Which confirms we're in the right place."

"Can you get us in, Master Kenobi?" you ask. "It could be difficult . . ."

"HA! I like a challenge!" he barks, dropping to his knees and feeling under the door, all the while mumbling darkly to himself.

While Kenobi tries to get the door open, you wander the hallways checking for signs of the battle still raging outside the monastery, but inside all is quiet.

You're about to return, when you hear the sound of some doors sliding open.

Who's that? you think, your heart thumping hard in your chest. It might be the doors just opening by themselves, but it could be someone, or something.

In the silence you creep along and peep around the corner . . .

Ventress and her battle droid bodyguards! I must warn Master Kenobi quickly!

You suddenly see Obi-Wan Kenobi round a corner and come marching toward you.

"Wrong way, youngling," he calls, all smiles. "I've just primed the charges to blow the door off. They're just about to explode . . . what is it?"

But you don't have to explain as the battle droids commence attack.

"Ventress!" you cry loudly, rushing fast down the hallway. "Ventress is with them!"

"Be calm," Kenobi orders, his voice soothing you. "Take cover and use your blaster. Do not panic—Ventress will use your weakness to destroy you!"

Flying past Kenobi, who uses his lightsaber to deflect the droid fire while you make it to safety, you round the corner from which he just came, and, out of the direct line of attack, you draw your blaster and prepare to fight the enemy.

Over the sound of the pitched battle in the hallway, you unexpectedly become aware of a faint *TINK-TINK-TINK* . . .

Outside the door of the chamber, you see Kenobi's primed charges counting down: 10, 9, 8, 7 . . .

If you join Obi-Wan Kenobi in the hallway and take on the best of the Separatist Army's trained assassins, turn to page 180.

If you can outpace the charges and make it safely to the opposite end of the hallway, click on box 1 on-screen and type code word RUN, or turn to page 38.

"You're right, Master Kenobi," you say, turning back to face him. "We need to put down the Separatist movement or on every planet there will be scenes played out such as the ones that occurred here today. I want to help the Republic destroy the Separatists . . . I will come with you."

Kenobi looks at you and nods his head.

"Well, youngling," he says, suddenly businesslike. "A Jedi's mission is not all lightsaber duels and blowing up castles! We must get to work."

The transport lands and you help the clone troopers load their fellow freedom fighters on to the ship. All the while searching for signs of Peder, but with no luck, there's no sight of him.

He must not have made it up this far, you think, gazing down from the ramparts out over the jungle. *Hopefully he's down there somewhere, safe and well and . . . probably looking for me!*

When the transport is loaded to capacity, you jump on board and watch as Teth gets smaller and smaller, finally disappearing as you enter thick cloud cover.

In a few moments, you're above the clouds and looming up before you is the enormous Jedi cruiser *Spirit of the Republic*.

"Whoa!" you exclaim loudly, to the amusement of the clone troopers around you.

"She's some ship, huh?" says one of them, laughing.

"Really incredible . . ." you reply, as you watch the transport dock with the cruiser.

As soon as the ship lowers its exit ramp, a platoon of medical droids file on board and take charge of the wounded.

"Come along with me, youngling," says Obi-Wan, suddenly appearing at your side. "We must see to your future."

As you walk, you listen as Kenobi tells you something of what you can expect if you decide to choose the way of the Jedi.

"It's the most difficult choice you'll make in your life," he says seriously. "And not one to be taken lightly. There is much training and a good deal of self-denial required of you."

You must look frightened because he smiles and quickly adds, "And your decision need not be made right now! I am forgetting myself. You must be tired. I will take you along to the sleeping quarters."

He escorts you to your pod and just as you're about to fall asleep, his departing words echo in your mind, "There are many ways you can help the Republic, youngling. Becoming a Jedi is just one of them."

In your dreams, you relive again the horrors of the monastery, and when you awaken, you have made the decision; you know which path you must choose . . .

If you follow the way of the Jedi, turn to page 165.
If you serve the Republic in your own way, turn to page 27.

"And you think that Jabba the Hutt may be financing this superweapon?" you ask.

"I think it's possible," says Godalhi thoughtfully. "As I said before, the B'omarr monk monastery has often been used as a base by Jabba. In some circles it's known as Hutt Castle, and my spies tell me quite a few large shipments have been delivered there in recent times. I didn't think there was anything particularly sinister in it before, because it never occurred to me that the Separatists were involved."

Quar Rohk shuffles uneasily in his chair. Clearly, even the mention of the Hutt is making him uncomfortable. Or is it that he knows something more about the clandestine deliveries?

"But now," says Godalhi, not seeming to notice the Trandoshan's discomfort. "I think it will be worth our while visiting the monastery to see for ourselves what were in those shipments."

"And how do you propossse we get inssside without either the Ssseparatissstsss or the Republicanssss ssseeing?" asks Rohk, doubtfully.

"Just leave that to me," says Godalhi mischievously. "Shall we go?"

The three of you return to Raidos New Library and make your way back along the hidden corridor to the monastery.

When you come to the turbolifts at the end, Godalhi turns to you both. "The hallways and chambers inside the monastery have been designed in a way to confuse and disorient unauthorized visitors. All the hallways look alike and it's easy to get lost, so stay close to me."

Entering the turbolift, you warn Godalhi of the previous problem you had with it and he removes the cover of the control panel and fiddles around with some wiring. When the turbolift begins its ascent, it's in a much more controlled manner than last time you were inside!

"We need to find a comlink," says Godalhi. "I can hack into it and hopefully we'll discover some clue as to what we're looking for."

When the doors slide open, you find yourself in a long, gloomy hallway and, stepping out, you follow behind Godalhi, with Rohk bringing up the rear. You stumble upon a fallen clone trooper in one of the many hallways and frisk him for weapons, pocketing a handful of detonation devices.

"You can never be too sure," you say, winking at Rohk. You soon locate a comlink and, after a few minor modifications, Godalhi manages to hack into the system.

"What I'm going to do," explains Godalhi without looking up from the screen, "is look at all the security measures that are currently in place throughout the monastery. If there's any chamber that has what seems to be an unwarranted level of security surrounding it, it'll probably hold what we're searching for."

You glance at Rohk who nervously shuffles from foot to foot.

He could simply be nervous knowing that the Separatists could stumble upon us at any time, you think, *or there's something more to his behavior . . .*

"Got it," whispers Godalhi suddenly, interrupting your thoughts. "There's a chamber on a lower level that is positively overloaded with the very latest security technology."

Re-entering the turbolift, you descend to a lower level and when you exit the lift you remark on its similarity to the level you were just on.

"It's as I said," says Godalhi. "The floor plans are exactly the same on every level, which in itself is a security system."

You hurry along the hallway and Godalhi suddenly stops outside a chamber door that looks very much like all the others you've passed, with the exception of a security panel set ingeniously into the wall.

"Subtle," says Godalhi admiringly, removing the panel's cover and adjusting some internals. "If we hadn't known already that this chamber was in some way important, we would have walked straight past it!"

"If this is the most up-to-date security system, what makes you think we can actually get in?" you ask him.

"Because," he replies, as the doors slide open. "I invented it!"

Turn to page 53.

"You've got to help me!" you yell desperately, looking up at the compactor and willing it to malfunction. "I can see these worker droids really look up to you, they respect you," you splutter. "You're like their god or something!"

Two other worker droids have joined their colleagues and are desperately trying to jam you in the bin. You have mere seconds left!

"Their god? My, my, how interesting. Do you think?" begins M-2XR excitedly. "Well perhaps I can try to convince them to . . ."

CA-CHUNK! CA-CHUNK! CA-CHUNK!

". . . let you go . . . oh—too late!"

THE END

The bodyguard brandishing the blaster doesn't look like someone you'll be able to reason with, so with your eyes glued to the barrel of his blaster, you yell out as loudly as you can.

"Senator Amidala! I come to you with news that the Separatists are planning on building a superweapon as big as a moon! I have just arrived from my homeworld of Teth where I aided Master Obi-Wan Kenobi, who also knows of this weapon."

You see the Senator look over her shoulder again.

"Let the youngling approach, Captain," she calls.

You move toward her and you see that beneath her authoritative manner, she seems worried about something.

"You have news of Master Kenobi? Or perhaps Anakin Skywalker?" she asks, concern clearly in her voice.

"I know that Master Kenobi has left Teth and is on his way to join Master Skywalker," you say respectfully. "That's as much as I know, but it's the Separatists' superweapon of which I wished to speak to you."

You see her visibly relax.

"Of course, please join me in my transport and you can tell me on the way to my next appointment," she says boarding the ship.

Turn to page 129.

My head . . . what just happened?!

You come to and find yourself lying on the floor of a massive, columned chamber. Gradually recovering, you get slowly to your feet, looking around for a clue that might tell you what just happened.

Maybe I fainted? you wonder doubtfully. *But if that were the case, someone must've moved me, because I wasn't in this room earlier . . .*

You check the doors of the chamber, but they're all locked.

"So I probably fainted, had a weird out-of-body experience, and then was brought here by some unknown person or thing," you say to yourself, scratching your head. Even after you've said it out loud, it still seems absurd!

"It's not so strange, youngling," you hear someone say and a hooded figure suddenly appears from behind one of the columns dotted around the chamber.

"Who are you?" you ask, recoiling from the approaching figure. Even though you've never been Force-sensitive, you can feel the evil surrounding the advancing form.

"I am Count Dooku!" Dooku booms, shrugging off his cowl and revealing his face.

Count Dooku! He'll never let you out of here alive . . . but you can't give up yet! You've been in many perilous situations today and you've made it this far!

"Yes, you are still alive and that is precisely why I've brought you here," says Dooku, coming to stand beside you.

The Force! He's using the Force to read your mind!

"Ah, youngling, your every thought is an open book to me," he says, chuckling slightly.

"You brought me here? Why?" you ask, confused.

"My servant Asajj Ventress recognized special hidden talents in you, youngling," he replies thoughtfully. "You have a high midi-chlorian count and have potential. Your courage and your intelligence have served you well thus far. The question is, do you have the courage and the intelligence to see the wisdom in the proposal I am about to offer you?"

"Which is?" you ask defiantly, throwing your head back and staring the old man in the eye.

"It is this: Join me and begin training as a Sith! You have the capabilities . . . you just need the discipline," replies Dooku.

"And if I refuse?" you ask, trying as hard as you can to keep your mind blank to avoid Dooku reading your thoughts and insecurities.

"If you refuse, I shall take your brain and your heart and create the next generation of cyborgs with you as their template!" says Dooku in reply.

If you join the Sith Order, turn to page 152.
If you would rather become a cyborg, turn to page 44.

"On your feet! Hands where I can see 'em," the clone trooper orders. You slowly stand and raise your hands above your head, Peder following suit.

"We're Tethans . . ." you begin to say, but the trooper isn't listening, he's already on his comlink.

"Captain, it appears I've found two young Tethans in the jungle near the base of the mesa, over," he reports, eyeing you doubtfully.

The comlink crackles and a voice replies. "Copy that, escort them back to the gunship for questioning, over."

"This way," the trooper says, gesturing with his blaster the way he wants you to walk.

CRA-ACK! A Separatist STAP fighter explodes and crashes to the ground seventy feet in front of you, its blaster cannons silenced.

Unhurt, the battle droid pilot clambers onto its feet, droid blaster drawn and ready.

In the confusion, two things happen at once . . .

"Come on, let's get out of here!" you hear Peder yell as he cartwheels out of the battle droid's line of fire, just as the clone trooper orders you to: "Hit the ground!"

If you follow Peder's lead, turn to page 166.
If you follow the Clone Trooper's order, turn to page 117.

The corridor stretches on and on . . . there's no end in sight!

You venture forth, careful to keep an eye out for security measures that may alert someone to your presence. After an hour, you reach another set of turbolifts, identical to the ones back at the monastery. Ensuring that they're in good working order, you enter cautiously.

Again the doors shut and before you know it, you're flying upward. *What's it with the turbolifts today?* you think, cursing your bad luck. Once again the doors slide open and standing before you is an old man.

"You took your time," he says, shaking your hand and grinning.

"Who are you? And where am I?" you blurt out in surprise. "How could you know I was coming?"

"I'm Janu Godalhi," he says, "and now not another word. We'll find somewhere to talk properly where you must tell me what's happening at the B'omarr monk monastery!"

You stare at him suspiciously, fearful of this seemingly gentle man.

"You did come from there, didn't you?" asks Godalhi, hustling you down the passageway away from the turbolifts.

Turn to page 85.

I've somehow got to retrieve the information now! you think desperately. Before the computer blows up, allowing whoever is responsible for this horrifying weapon to escape justice!

You race over to the speeder and find some tools stashed in a compartment under the seat and, selecting one of them, you jam it under the comlink cover to pry it open.

If I can just stop this endless loop . . .

But that's the last thing you ever think as blasts of electricity shoot through your body.

THE END

Not a moment too soon! you say to yourself as you wipe sweat off your forehead. I was about to get pummeled by a giant woolly behemoth!

"You're a hero, you are," says a kindly Bith, patting you on the back.

"Not many that would go up against a Wookiee," someone else adds.

Pretty soon, everyone is congratulating you!

"Oh really, it was nothing. Anybody would have done the same," you say modestly.

"But that's where you're wrong, youngling," says a reassuringly calm voice at your side. "I saw what happened, you showed great courage."

Master Glynn-Beti, you'd recognize her anywhere!

"I-I-I . . . thank you, Master," you say, tongue-tied and embarrassed.

"Now that you've charmed these good people with your gallantry," says Master Glynn-Beti, lowering her voice and giving you a wink. "Perhaps you could help the Jedi by escorting them to their ships."

Me? Help the Jedi?

Incoming Separatist fire rocks the corridor.

"And be quick about it," she adds. "There is much work for you to do!"

THE END

You watch helplessly as Kenobi battles against the evil Ventress.

Quickly you draw your weapon and fire at Ventress, who deftly deflects the lasers with her lightsabers, leaving Obi-Wan free to roll out of the way and retrieve his weapon.

"Another one of your little tame pets?" snarls Ventress. Force-jumping off a column, Kenobi reignites his lightsaber and somersaults back to land at Ventress's feet, bringing the weapon down on her shoulder.

"No, but a very welcome diversion all the same," he replies, chuckling.

Quickly Ventress blocks Kenobi's strike and leaps out of the window!

Kenobi jumps onto the windowsill, and waves his lightsaber in your direction, "I will catch up with you, youngling!" he yells, before springing out.

In the sudden quiet of the empty chamber, you hear the bang and crash of battle droids descending the stairs . . . they're coming down to this level!

If you follow Kenobi and Ventress, turn to page 125.

If you keep one step ahead of the droid attack, click on box G on-screen and type code word STEP, or turn to page 21.

The best thing I can do is stay inside this gunship, you tell yourself calmly, trying to fight the fear that's rising in the pit of your stomach.

It's got to have some kind of special defense shield, doesn't it?

Outside, you hear the roar of the STAP fighters buzzing overhead, their cannons blazing and the sound of return fire from the clone troopers taking cover in the clearing.

A huge explosion tilts the gunship and, losing your balance, you slide underneath the desk the clone captain was sitting at minutes before.

K-K-KIIIIK! The transparisteel screen buckles and shatters into a million pieces. Luckily you're sheltered from the worst of the shards.

"Sector 6574-A, incoming!" you hear Plo Koon yell and you wonder how the troopers can remember all the codes they have to memorize, before realizing you've answered your own question: They're clones.

"The Tethan is in there!" you hear someone shrieking from outside and you're suddenly aware that that's the last thing you'll ever hear . . .

THE END

No, that's right, I don't! you think angrily, refusing to follow Obi-Wan as he disappears around a corner. Although that's exactly what you expect me to do, isn't it? Well I've made it this far on my own . . .

Stomping down the hallway in the opposite direction, your face red with anger, you know you've made the right decision.

It'd take forever to check all these hallways. They all look the same. You'd just be going around in circles!

As you turn yet another corner, you see Ventress stalking up the hallway in your direction.

"Oh, if it isn't Kenobi's little shadow," she calls out.

"I thought you'd gone!" you say, your voice quavering in fear, as you dive for a door through which to escape.

"It's trying to run, how quaint," she purrs, Force-pulling the door closed. "No, I haven't gone anywhere!"

Now she's upon you, her face just inches from yours.

"I feel your anger, youngling," smirks Ventress, staring into your eyes. "Let me help you avenge yourself on Kenobi . . ."

"I'll never help you!" you screech, fighting to turn your head from her insistent gaze, but it's impossible! Her eyes consume you.

"Oh . . . but you will . . . you will . . ." she whispers.

THE END

"If you don't tell these droids right now that it was your translation error and I didn't actually call them 'galactic goons,'" you scream, the sweat pouring down your face, "I am contacting your makers, Cybot Galactica, and telling them that you refused to help!"

"But if you do that, they'll have my entire line recalled and have us all destroyed!" it says, panic-stricken.

"YES! YES THEY WILL! NOW TELL THEM TO LET ME GO!"

M-2XR immediately starts bleeping at the worker droids who unhand you instantly and you fall to the floor, panting for breath.

CA-CHUNK! CA-CHUNK! CA-CHUNK!

"There, that was easy, wasn't it?" burbles M-2XR. "No need to bother Cybot Galactica at all. Everything is completely sorted . . . oh, the youngling has fainted! That's enough of an adventure for you today!"

THE END

You've found help!

It's Jedi Master Obi-Wan Kenobi, who, using his lightsaber, easily deflects the barrage of fire from the pursuing droideka.

"Step on it, youngling," Kenobi yells, scrambling onboard the speeder. "There are too many of them, you need to get us out of here right now!"

Accelerating down the hallways, the droideka right behind you, you both see a bank of turbolifts up ahead.

"Pull in close to the turbolift control panel!" Kenobi bellows loudly over the sound of cannon fire. "I'll call a lift, then we'll take the speeder around the passageways and quickly double back here as fast as we can. By that time, the lift doors should be open and we can lose these metallic monsters that way."

You nod your head and swerve close to the control panel so Obi-Wan can execute his plan.

Turning left and then another hard left, you end up back at the lifts, but you've taken too long to do it. The turbolift doors are closing!

"The gap between the doors is too small, we'll never make it!" you scream, closing your eyes.

Turn to page 36.

As more STAPs begin bombarding the site, you turn to the captain. "I know a secret way in!" you say. "I can show you where it is."

The captain nods, and after shouting a few orders to his men, he indicates you should follow him, as he runs across the open ground of the base to the shelter of the trees, with you right behind him.

"Where are we heading, kid?" asks the clone captain.

"Around here to the right at the base of the mesa," you reply.

Keeping low under the shelter of the overhang, you've traveled about a mile when you see somebody up ahead, lying among the dirt and dried leaves.

You dart forward and, as you near, you see it's Peder!

"Peder, are you okay?" you say, rushing as fast as you can to his side, the clone captain following.

Kneeling beside him, the captain checks Peder's vital signs.

"He's okay. He's just unconscious. This rock fall looks recent," he says, glancing around at the rocks and stones that litter the small clearing. "He must've gotten hit on the head. He'll be fine, although we should get him to a medical droid now. I'll take him back to base and be right back."

"But the STAP fighters?" you say, alarmed.

"Just let me handle that," the captain replies, effortlessly scooping up Peder and disappearing around the side of the cliff.

In the distance, you hear STAPs still bombarding the

base and now that you're on your own, you begin to shiver uncontrollably with fear.

Telling yourself to stay calm, you distract yourself by looking for the secret turbolift. Thick vines cover this area of the cliff face, but you and Peder would play around here as younglings and it doesn't take you long to find what you're looking for. Stripping the vines off, you're surprised—and relieved—to see that the turbolift is in working order.

Peder must've come here in search of the turbolift straight after he disappeared. *If only I'd gone with him . . .*

But there's no time for recriminations when you suddenly hear the sound of footsteps approaching noisily through the undergrowth, and around the corner of the cliff you see a huge super battle droid!

It hasn't seen me yet, you think, backing up slowly until you're pressed hard up against the turbolift door. Reaching out your arm, you open the doors and back in.

The sound of the doors opening has alerted the super battle droid to your presence and he fires a blaster bolt which luckily glances off the doors just as they're closing!

The lift immediately begins to descend and you see that the control panel inside is damaged, but it stops as mysteriously as it started and when the doors open, you get out and find yourself in a long, dark corridor . . .

Turn to page 103.

Over Ventress's shoulder, you see five or six clone troopers speeding toward you. A feeling of relief sweeps over you. But it's not over yet!

With Ventress distracted, you drop your shoulder and throw yourself as hard as you can into her exposed side, your shoulder and elbow crashing heavily into her ribs. Luckily you keep your footing and, although you haven't knocked her over, it's enough to make Ventress let go.

Now is your chance! Moving across the quadrangle, you hit the monastery doorway in seconds flat, almost skidding over on the polished stone floor. *She hasn't followed me!* you think to yourself thankfully. *She must have her hands full with the clones.*

You're about to head toward an inner doorway to your right, when you hear the ominous sound of marching feet and dart behind a column just as the thin, rigid bodies of a squadron of battle droids file through the door.

That must be her regular goon squad, you think and, catching sight of their soulless eyes, you're grateful she was alone when she stumbled upon you in the quadrangle. Once they've passed, you dash to the door through which they just came and bump straight into a destroyer droid!

Turn to page 18.

You gaze around enviously at the other patrons enjoying the many wonders the cantina has to offer, from playing games to dancing.

Suddenly a strange-looking trader catches your eye and smiles in a friendly fashion, raising his cup to you.

You return his smile distractedly and continue looking around at the surrounding mayhem.

There are so many species here! Is that a Staglint? you wonder, watching a twenty-armed, blue creature on the dance floor with a beautiful Bothan female.

Then, from the corner of your eye, you see the trader again raising his cup and signaling for you to come over and join him.

Do I know this guy? Is he signaling to me? you wonder, looking at the trader again and pointing to yourself. He nods and beckons you over again.

"I noticed you sitting there," he says, laughing as you slip into a seat beside him. "You look out of place! I'm Pwi'lin, by the way."

"You can say that again," you reply and introduce yourself. Soon you're chatting like friends (albeit ones who fail to mention the reason why they're in Raidos!), when you are interrupted by Pwi'lin's comlink.

"Errruka?" says Pwi'lin, in his own language. "Rindath con fa'alen deasant? Okay, poodarn."

"That was my first mate," he says. "He's made the repairs to my ship, so I must join him at the spaceport," he adds. "We've had some problems getting parts for the *Rindoon Dart*—that's my ship, she's a Sandonian 4XA Prensile cruiser—from the merchants here on Teth, who only seem to have old stock for the clunkers they ordinarily service."

"A Sandonian 4XA Prensile Cruiser—the fastest ship in the Galaxy!" you say, excitedly.

"You have heard of this ship?" asks Pwi'lin in a surprised voice.

"We may be a backwater planet," you grin, "but the occasional bit of news filters down to us from the rest of the galaxy."

"Well if you want to accompany me as far as the spaceport, you can see her," he says. "Though I won't have time to show you around."

"Really?" you cry. "Great! I must tell my companion I'm going, though."

"Of course," says Pwi'lin, looking forward to showing off his ship.

With the usual warnings about hurrying back and "I'm not waiting around forever for you!" you and Pwi'lin slip out the cantina door.

Turn to page 189.

You know that Godalhi is probably right, his shouted warnings have made you wary. You stop running, and instead try calling out to the wounded creature.

"Hello, can I help you? Are you okay?" you call out.

There's no response and the sound of approaching footsteps is getting louder . . .

"Come back! Someone's coming!" you hear Peder plaintively cry.

You stand there for a moment, torn between helping the creature and returning to your friend.

"Come on!" Peder calls again.

What am I going to do for it? I need Godalhi's help! If he has a medpac, I can tend to the wounded thing while he holds off the . . . well, whatever it is that's coming!

"All right, all right, I'm coming!" you yell back, your mind made up. You rush back down the corridor to Peder and Godalhi, relief showing plainly on both their faces.

"Now get in that room!" Godalhi orders. "You two need to hide! We don't know what's coming down the corridor, but we need to be ready!"

Turn to page 146.

Caught in the cross fire between a battle droid and a clone trooper, you don't need to be told twice to hit the ground!

DOOW-DOOW-DOOW!

You've barely flung yourself down when you hear the crushing sound of the battle droid falling onto the twisted remains of its STAP fighter and, next thing you know, the trooper is pulling you to your feet and asking if you're okay.

"Uh, I guess so," you reply uncertainly, and looking around you suddenly remember Peder's escape plan.

"Where did my friend go?" you ask the trooper worriedly.

"He ran off into the bushes. He's all right, you can catch up with him later, but right now you're coming with me," replies the trooper. "And don't even think about trying to make a run for it, okay?"

You nod your head in agreement and the clone trooper holsters his blaster and leads the way back to his command post.

Turn to page 50.

You stand still, frozen with indecision, and listen to sounds of Rohk laughing excitedly and banging around the room.

Abruptly, the sounds stop and Rohk pops his head out.

"It's sssafe," he says. "I have disssabled the sssecurity sssysssstem."

Seeing your hesitation, the Trandoshan laughs.

"Vigilance is a credit to you," he says. "But there is nothing to fear."

You take a few steps and you're at the doorway. Inside you see that the chamber is stacked to the ceiling with metal crates!

Quar Rohk produces a blaster from his cloak and fires at the nearest crate. The blast ricochets off it and bounces around the room! You both drop to the floor and it's luck that neither of you are injured.

"What are you doing?" you yell, from your position on the floor.

The Trandoshan's green skin darkens slightly in some sort of blush.

"Sssorry, youngling," he says bashfully. "I ssshould have realized it wasssn't going to be ssso eassssy to break open thessse chessstsss."

He places the blaster on a crate and resumes rummaging around in his cloak, this time revealing a set of tools, none of which you recognize.

You watch as he gets to work on trying to get a crate open.

"Are you a thief?" you ask, timidly, not wishing to offend someone who saved your life twice.

"Amongssst other thingsss," he says, grunting with effort.

You hear a sound and Rohk gives a rumble of satisfaction.

"Ssssimple," he says, slowly raising the lid of the crate.

"Too ssssimple!" says a voice. You see a woman smiling.

"Ventresssss!" squeaks Rohk, dropping the lid of the crate in shock.

Turn to page 150.

That split-second diversion gives you enough time to pull a thermal detonator from your tunic, just as Ventress turns to face you.

"Your naive friends behind me think they can save you, youngling," she smiles, strengthening her grip on your shoulder. "But you know the old saying: A Tethan in the hand is worth four clone troopers in a randoos bush!"

"I don't think so, Ventress," you reply angrily, holding up the detonation device for her to see.

For a moment, her eyes widen in fear as she watches the timer ticking down, but she quickly recovers her composure.

"Although I wanted the pleasure of killing you myself, I see you have your own ideas," says Ventress, spinning you around to stand between her and the troopers, she keeps an eye on the timer.

5 . . . 4 . . . 3 . . .

Suddenly Ventress Force-throws you into the midst of the clone troopers who have been watching from a distance!

2 . . . 1 . . . *KAA-BOOOOOM!*

THE END

I can't win this!

You take a few steps back as Ventress nears and, turning, you race as fast as you can down the hallway.

Suddenly, your feet leave the floor and you're rising slowly into the air.

"Foolish human!" shrieks Ventress. "Did you really think you could outrun me?"

Using the Force, Ventress slowly reels you in and you know your time has come . . .

THE END

As you make your way through the jungle toward the mesa, you wonder where Peder could be. It seems funny now that you'd tried to warn him about the dangers associated with running headlong into battle—like getting yourself killed!—when that's exactly what you've ended up doing!

Well . . . not funny exactly, you think to yourself, wiping your bloody face on the sleeve of your tunic.

You hear an insistent buzzing and, looking up, you spy a fresh squadron of STAPs fly over the treetops, heading in the direction of the clone trooper base you've just fled.

May the Force be with you, Plo Koon! you say to yourself, hoping that he'll make it out alive.

You're only about three hundred feet from the foot of the mesa when you hear, from in front of you, the metallic crunch of an AT-TE grinding to a halt and you duck down into some thick bushes to scope out what is happening.

There are only a handful of clone troopers left in the clearing, the rest having already scaled the craggy precipice to launch their assault on the B'omarr monk monastery.

It's then you notice how quiet it is!

The troopers must've taken out the Separatists' laser cannons! you realize gleefully. *I can't wait to get up there and help!* But it's the "getting up there" that could be a problem!

The troopers had ascension cables to help them scale the vertical cliff and, although there are plenty of vines covering the craggy face, it looks a little too dangerous for a complete novice to try.

In a quiet corner of the clearing, you spot a medical

droid tending an injured trooper. Having removed the clone's helmet and placed it on top of a large boulder, the medical droid is now scanning the trooper's limbs to assess the extent of his injuries.

Ahhh, just what I'm looking for, you murmur to yourself. The trick is to swoop down by the boulder, scoop up the helmet, and keep walking like nothing has happened. Like taking camby berries from an Ewok!

You put your plan into action and everything seems to be going fine . . . until you hear someone shouting behind you! You're not even certain they're yelling at you and, instead of turning around, you shove the helmet on your head and march purposefully toward the AT-TE.

"Hey, you!" You hear the sound of running feet, but you don't break your stride.

By the time you reach the closest leg of the AT-TE, it's about to begin the long ascent to the top of the mesa and you launch yourself at the foot of the colossal weapon and hang on!

Turn to page 167.

You know you don't have a chance on your own! You watch the troopers approaching and wonder how you can get their attention without getting your head blasted off!

When the colossal foot of an AT-TE thunders down feet from your hideout, you jump to your feet, giving a surprised yelp. That's all the troopers need, they've quickly got you in their sights and you slowly raise your hands above your head.

"I'm a Tethan, please don't shoot!" you call out loudly.

You're staring down the barrels of several blasters and you feel your knees wobbling with fear. One of the clones activates his comlink, while the others continue to point their blasters at your head.

"We've found a Tethan, sir," reports the clone. "What are our orders?"

For a split second, the fizzle of dead air fills the space between you and the blasters, then the response comes through. "Bring the Tethan in for questioning, out."

"Roger, Captain," the clone buzzes. "This way," he says, using his blaster to point the way that they've just come.

Turn to page 50.

Sprinting to the window, you see Obi-Wan and Ventress below you, still locked in combat!

Then, with a quick jerking movement, Kenobi flicks the lightsaber out of Ventress's right hand and it goes flying.

"Jedi scum!" Ventress shrieks and, as a vulture droid swoops down, she jumps on and flies out of sight.

"Wait for me there, youngling. I'll be along in a moment," Obi-Wan calls as he reenters the monastery.

Running to the entrance, you see battle droids moving along the hallway. Deciding not to wait around to be discovered, you sneak out of the room and creep along the hallway in the opposite direction until you stumble upon a bank of turbolifts.

The doors open and Kenobi stands there, surprised.

"Hello, looking for me?" he says, about to exit the lift.

The battle droids, hearing Kenobi's voice, open fire!

"Blast!" says Kenobi, grabbing you by the arm and hauling you into the turbolift, but the doors don't close.

"The doors are stuck!" you shout as a battle droid appears. Then a second battle droid, then a third . . .

Turn to page 161.

You land heavily on the dirt floor and manage to quickly get to your feet to face your enemy.

There's a huge gate drawn halfway up to your right and from behind it you can hear the snuffles and snorts of the approaching horror. It's not a trick! The rancor must've been scared off by the sounds of the falling crates, but it's only a matter of time before it returns to investigate!

To your left, you see a small, wooden door with a metal grill in it and, rushing over to open it, you see Ventress's face peering through the bars.

Suddenly you hear a gigantic roar behind you and the rancor lumbers into view, its huge arms stretched out before it, its razor-sharp claws pawing at the half-open gate!

"That gate will hold until I finish you off, youngling!" screams Ventress, as she enters the chamber and ignites her lightsaber. "Then, dead or half-dead, you will make a tasty morsel for the beast!"

Turn to page 84.

"I can't do it," you say softly, shifting painfully on the dirt floor.

"Then there is nothing I can do for you, youngling," Ventress replies, helping you into a more comfortable position. "Except to take you out of this lair and leave you somewhere where the clone troopers might find you in time . . ."

She easily picks you up and carries you out of the chamber, through a series of hallways, and out onto the ramparts of the monastery into the open air. Depositing you where there's a chance you'll be discovered, she leaves you without another word.

Above you, you see Jedi starfighters battling the Separatist war machines and you know that whatever happens now, you were right to deny the dark side.

THE END

"No way!" you say angrily. "That's not a fair swap. If you know where to find Janu Godalhi, just tell us."

The Barabel sentries laugh uproariously and you realize you have no hope of either getting the information you need or being allowed to enter the city now that you've refused the option to bribe them.

Red-faced and angry, you and Peder mount your speeder bikes and turn in the direction of home, the sound of Barabel insults ringing in your ears.

"Go homesssss, the city issssssssss no place for younglingssssssss!"

THE END

On the way, you tell Senator Amidala all that has befallen you since the previous morning, her bodyguards leaning forward, eagerly enthralled by your tale.

"You certainly have had some adventures," Amidala says smiling at you. "And I thank you for coming to me with this most valuable intelligence. In fact, I'm meeting with someone right now who will find this information most interesting, I'm sure . . ."

The transport draws up to a skyway and you see Jedi Master Mace Windu awaiting the arrival of the Senator.

"You have a meeting with Master Windu?" you ask excitedly.

"Why, yes I do. Would you like to meet him?" she asks laughing, then quickly adds. "Before my guards escort you back to your ship?"

"Certainly, Senator," you reply coolly, acting as if hanging out with Jedi is something you do on a regular basis.

Senator Amidala sees right through you, laughing delightedly and, as the transport doors slide open, you hear her introduction.

"Master Windu, please allow me to introduce to you one of the most courageous young people I've ever met," Amidala says.

THE END

You don't like the sound of this "you as the bait" plan, but the rancor is still blocking the exit, your one chance of fleeing the chamber.

"Okay," you yell. "But if we make it out of this, you have to let me go!"

Ventress nods her head briefly in agreement and continues striking at the rancor.

"I'm going to put away my weapon!" she yells. "I want you to stand on top of those crates and draw the rancor's attention and then I'll slip behind it and stab its vulnerable spot between the two armored plates on its neck!"

"Right!" you yell, scrambling on top of the metal crates. Ventress immediately deactivates her lightsaber and you begin waving your arms at the rancor.

"Come on, you big, smelly fiend!" you scream. "Come and get me, you lumbering lunk!"

The rancor, confused by Ventress's unexpected retreat, lurches toward you, its massive arms swinging and its teeth bared in anger!

You see Ventress Force-leap onto its back and reignite her lightsaber, but it's too late, the rancor's lethal claws slice through the air and grab you around the waist, lifting you up toward its salivating maw!

You scream in pain and disgust as you're about to be devoured by the monster, when all of sudden it lets out an ear-piercing screech of its own as it staggers and slumps to the ground, mortally wounded by Ventress's blow.

You've done it! The rancor is dead!

You lie on the ground, still wrapped up in the dead beast's grip, gulping down air and unable to move.

You hear Ventress deactivate her lightsaber and jump off the still shuddering body of the rancor and the next moment she's pulling you out of its grasp and across the dirt floor.

"You showed great courage, youngling," she says, with something like respect. "But your injuries are grave, I don't know how much longer you will last."

"I'm dying?" you ask in a small voice.

"The rancor's claws have pierced your body," says Ventress quietly. "There is nothing I can do to save you. Only my Master, Count Dooku, can help you now . . ."

"Count Dooku?" you say, your voice trailing off.

"He can harness the powers of the dark side and he may be able to save your life," she says. "The choice is yours, youngling."

If you join the dark side in order to save your own life, turn to page 188.

If you would rather die than join the dark side, turn to page 127.

From your position facedown on the ground, you can't see who it is, but at least it's not a security droid!

"Stay where you are," whispers the voice. "A security droid is coming."

"Are you Raan Calrissian, sir?" asks a security droid.

"Yes, I am," the voice replies. "I hope you're here to tell me you've finished pulling my ship apart!"

"I am, sir," replies the droid. "You're cleared for departure at Gate 134."

"That ship better be in the same condition as I left it!" grunts Calrissian sternly.

The droid departs, and Raan Calrissian ducks behind the crates to inspect your security bracelets.

"Easy," you hear him mutter and he quickly picks them, you're free!

"Thanks," you say removing the gag and rubbing your arms until you feel the blood circulating again.

"No problem," replies Calrissian nonchalantly. "You've got a lot of guts, kid. You're just lucky I was the only one who saw you exit that transport."

He helps you to your feet and you're surprised (and grateful) that he's not bombarding you with questions on why you were tied up!

"Well, I'd better get moving," says Calrissian, looking you up and down to check that you're okay. "Be careful now. And stay away from any unscrupulous types. Like that posse of Jedi I saw hanging around here just before you 'dropped' in! HA!"

He's still snickering over his parting comment as he turns and leaves to board his ship.

With nothing better to do, you wander out of the loading bay and find a viewing platform. With your nose pressed up against the cool transparisteel, you look up and see Cloud City's upper levels, hovering far above you.

It's so beautiful, you think, as you watch the steady stream of ships entering and exiting Cloud City's many spaceports, *no wonder they have so many visitors here!*

While you're gazing out at the traffic, you see a Separatist cruiser abruptly drop beneath the thick clouds that give Cloud City its name and you watch, horrified, as the ship disgorges its fighters, which then move into battle formation!

Cloud City is under attack! *Oh no! Not again!* you think, panic rising in your chest. *What am I going to do?*

If you find Raan Calrissian and hitch a ride out on his ship, turn to page 49.

If you find the Jedi Calrissian spoke of and appeal for help, turn to page 136.

If you hide somewhere and blast as many Separatist bloodworms as you can before they find you, click on box F on-screen and type code word HIDE, or turn to page 17.

You'll do things your own way or not at all! You know from experience that your elders tend to just pat you on the head in a patronizing way and ignore whatever you say.

The AT-TE is only about seventy feet from you now and closing, and the clone troopers are so close, you can clearly hear their comlinks cracking and popping with orders.

You need to decide what you're going to do now, before they stumble upon you by accident . . .

CRA-ACK!

Suddenly, your decision is made for you! The AT-TE, while forging its way through the jungle, has broken off a huge branch from the tree that hangs over the bushes where you're hiding and it comes tumbling down. You hear the fearful sound and look up just in time, flinging yourself out of your hiding place just as the branch crashes to the ground, flattening the bush under its weight.

But now you're lying on your back, frozen with fear, staring up at an enormous metal foot that's just about to come smashing down on your body and squash you into oblivion!

"Look out!" You hear a clone trooper yell the warning and it's enough to snap you out of your trance, and you roll out of the way of the foot as it pounds into the ground only inches from where you are lying.

You lay still with your eyes closed, trying to get your breath back, and realize that the clone troopers will be on you in a second and that your grand plan of going it alone will no longer be possible.

"On your feet," you hear a trooper bark and, opening your eyes, you see that you're surrounded by clones, their drawn blasters pointing right at you.

You sit up slowly, giving the troopers plenty of time to see you're unarmed, and look around weighing your options.

Behind you, the AT-TE you've just avoided being flattened by is moving inexorably forward through the jungle, but you can hear more on their way and can just make out the top of one coming toward you . . . it should be here any minute, you say to yourself, the glimmer of an escape plan forming in your mind . . .

"On your feet, I said," repeats the trooper, and this time the rest of the clones that have you surrounded lower their weapons and fall back, allowing you to clamber to your feet.

"I'm a Tethan youngling," you say in a small, pathetic voice, wishing you could fake some tears to add to your act. "I'm unarmed."

The approaching AT-TE lurches into the clearing and the clone troopers shuffle out of its oncoming path. And that's the moment you've been waiting for!

You fling yourself onto the foot of the metallic beast and, holding on tightly, it carries you high up into the air and away from the clones.

Turn to page 16.

Raan Calrissian said he saw Jedi! They'll help me!

Running back the way you came, you quickly hit a snag; hundreds of people have seen the incoming Separatist ships and are flocking to the spaceports to flee the attack. The crowd is packed shoulder-to-shoulder and are barely moving; you'll never find the Jedi.

You see a small Brindal girl stumble and fall as the crowd surges forward, desperate to make it past the security droids, who are using their weapons to maintain a semblance of control.

You watch for a moment, but the Brindal has yet to get to her feet! She'll be trampled if you don't do something.

"Hey!" you call at the top of your voice to anyone who'll listen. "Hey, look out! A Brindal child has fallen over, help her up!"

But the crowd isn't listening to you and you watch in horror as the huge gathering heaves forward again.

Without thinking, you throw yourself into the backs of those closest to you and burrow through the arms, legs, tails, and tentacles of the crowd, to reach the spot you saw the Brindal fall.

"Hey! Watch what you're doing!" someone yells, shoving you in the back, the only thing stopping you from falling is an enormous Wookiee, who turns and roars in your face.

You're starting to panic again; you have to get to the Brindal before it's too late, but it's impossible to get past the Wookiee blocking your passage through!

For a second, you're unsure what to do next, when suddenly you notice the elaborate hair adornments on the head of the person next to you.

Quick as a flash, you grab one of the combs and jab the sharp end right into the Wookiee's behind!

ROOOOOOOOOARARRRRRRRRRRR-OROROR!

As the Wookiee turns to grab you, you duck down and tunnel between his legs. The Wookiee, facing the front again, attempts to cuff you around the head with his massive hairy mitt, and everyone in the surrounding area ducks their head and moves out of the way!

You leap forward into the gap that has opened and rush toward the wailing Brindal, pulling her to her feet just as the Wookiee grabs you!

"WAAAIT!!" you scream, readying yourself for the knockout blow, and amazingly the crowd falls silent. Even the Brindal stops crying!

"I'm sorry I stabbed you with a comb," you say to the Wookiee. "I just had to get past you to rescue this Brindal. She'd fallen over and was going to get crushed if I didn't do something . . . drastic."

"WWWRAAAAAAROOO!" says the Wookiee, loosening his grip a little.

Over the roar, you hear voices rippling through the crowd: "The Jedi are here! The Jedi are here! We're saved!"

Turn to page 105.

Since when do ventilation shafts have a steep drop like this? you ask yourself as you continue falling. *Unless it's not a ventilation shaft and instead a rubbish shoot! I hope they're not jettisoning the junk!*

Using your legs you furiously try and brace yourself against the side of the shoot to keep from falling, but you can't find a foothold!

Luckily, when you finally catapult out the end, you're not spat out into space; rather you land heavily on a narrow conveyor belt traversing a seemingly bottomless pit leading to who-knows-where!

Surrounded by bits of smashed up droid, you lay very still, trying hard to fight the urge to look over the edge into the gaping maw below.

The conveyor belt stretches for another three hundred feet in front of you, collecting bits of junk from numerous other rubbish shoots along the way, and at the end you see a line of worker droids sorting through the parts coming off the conveyor belt.

A droid reprocessing plant! Oh, this isn't so bad, you think to yourself, putting the sheer drop to your left and right out of your mind.

If I can just get the attention of those droids, I'll ask them to turn off the conveyor belt and just walk very carefully to safety.

As you draw closer, you see that the worker droids are putting the rejected parts into a huge bin. Every thirty seconds, a giant metal compactor slams down on the junked pieces, flattening the scrap to the width of your hand. You try yelling over the noise of the compactor to get their attention.

"Hello! Here . . . on the conveyor belt," you call to the worker droids, waving your hands above your head. "A little help? Could you . . ."

CA-CHUNK! CA-CHUNK! CA-CHUNK!

". . . turn off the conveyor belt?"

Seeing you, they begin tooting animatedly away in their own language, but don't make any attempt to switch off the conveyor belt.

CA-CHUNK! CA-CHUNK! CA-CHUNK!

"Can. You. Turn. This. Off?" But it's no use, the droids are simple worker droids; they don't have the capacity to understand standard language.

CA-CHUNK! CA-CHUNK! CA-CHUNK!

"This is ridiculous! I could fall off this thing or get knocked off by all this blasted flying debris!" you yell at them in frustration, dodging a droid torso that has just flown out of a rubbish shoot and on to the conveyor belt.

CA-CHUNK! CA-CHUNK! CA-CHUNK!

To your surprise, the torso sits up and spins its head around to look straight at you.

"I'll have you know, I am not flying debris!" it says, its photoreceptors lighting up indignantly. "I'm protocol droid M-2XR and you are rude!"

Turn to page 30.

"While that may be true, Chancellor," she says calmly.
"We still do need to use diplomacy when dealing with other
Core Worlds to ensure . . ."

"Yes, yes, Senator," says Palpatine patronizingly, cutting
her off. "We've been over this before. We know your
distrust of the Rutanian Senatorial process and I don't think
we need to go over it again."

Senator Amidala bows her head. As you watch her, you
sense she has raised the issue of the Separatists many times
before and with nothing new to put before the Senate.

If I could just tell her what I know about the Separatists'
plans for the superweapon . . .

"We'd better go," says the guard nervously and you
follow him out.

Once outside, you ask him where you can find Senator
Amidala's office and he laughs wheezily.

"Do you see all those Senate Guards?" You nod your
head. "Well they're there to stop you from getting close to
the Senators!"

You thank the guard for showing you around and exit
the building, only to duck back inside once he's gone.

I must see the Senator, you think urgently.

Turn to page 158.

Hot, tired, and not a little scared, you finally arrive at your destination, and find a welcoming committee of one awaiting you.

"I am TC-70," says the golden protocol droid, bowing slightly. "Welcome to Jabba the Hutt's Palace. Please come this way."

She leads the way and you follow her deep into the cool interior of the Palace and, after a few twists and turns, you arrive at the main audience chamber.

In the middle of the room upon his dais, sits the grotesque Hutt, surrounded by his criminal minions!

The most famous—and the most ruthless—crime lord in the galaxy!

A hush descends over the room as you enter, the musicians in the corner silenced by a sign from the Hutt, and all eyes are on you.

"Ahhh, sleemo paadunko maka?" Jabba asks, his deep bass voice booming and echoing around the chamber.

You don't know how to speak Huttese, but TC-70 quickly translates.

"His eminence Jabba the Hutt would like to know what business you have here on Tatooine," she says.

"Please tell the great Jabba," you reply, "that I'm just visiting, having never been to Tatooine before, and that I know no one on this world."

"Zenhoo bala wowga peepu?" asks Jabba, his eyes suspicious.

"The mighty Jabba would like to know why you come

to Tatooine in a Credaan Spacer. A ship you could have only acquired from the Republican Army," says TC-70.

"Please tell the all-powerful Jabba that I borrowed the ship off of Master Obi-Wan Kenobi, who I was helping to fight the Separatists on my homeworld of Teth," you say, wondering how much you ought to mention about the battle.

"AHAHAAAAAHHHH!" Jabba laughs uproariously, his obsequious followers joining in. "Zeeda pookee mufia paalana!"

"The magnificent Jabba says he doubts very much a youngling like you would be of any use to a great Jedi such as Kenobi," says TC-70.

Your face burns redder with shame, as the entire chamber bursts into renewed bouts of hilarity at the sight of your humiliation.

"Well, you can tell the divine Jabba that I did more than merely help the Jedi, I told them some things that they wouldn't have discovered on their own. Like about the crystalline vertex ca . . ." Your voice dies out, as you immediately regret your angry outburst.

Every species in the room stops laughing and looks at Jabba; how is the ruthless Hutt going to repay such rudeness from a "guest"?

"Moota rewuu crystalline vertex bartoo? Graanda o tawntee!" he says, leaning forward with interest.

"The most gracious Jabba would like to know more about the crystalline vertex on Teth," says TC-70. "You will tell him or die."

If I tell Jabba the Hutt that the crystalline vertex cache was blown up, he'll probably have me killed immediately, you think desperately. *But if I tell him that it's still there, there's a slim chance he may take me with him back to Teth to retrieve it, and I might get a chance to escape . . .*

If you tell Jabba that the Republican Army destroyed the crystalline vertex cache, turn to page 31.

If you tell Jabba that the crystalline vertex cache is still on Teth, turn to page 176.

You spin around one hundred and eighty degrees and standing about one hundred and fifty feet away from you, is a tall, thin woman, a hood drawn up over her head. From beneath the hood, you see two malevolent eyes staring out at you, and even from this distance you can see they're full of hatred and fury.

Casting a glance over your shoulder, you see that the destroyer droid, hearing the newcomer's voice, has also turned its attention on you!

"What's that? Nexu got your tongue?" she says, grinning evilly and drawing a pair of lightsabers out from under her cloak. "It'll have to fight me for it!"

Out of the corner of your eye, you see a door into the monastery.

If only you could make it to that door, then you could lose yourself in the darkness!

But the doorway seems a very long, long way away . . .

If you lob the detonation device at the woman, turn to page 22.

If you try to blow up the destroyer droid, turn to page 65.

If you make a run for the monastery door, turn to page 169.

"So it does exist!" you say, looking over to where he's pointing and seeing the closed doors of the turbolift, still partially hidden by thick, hanging vines.

"Yeah," says Peder excitedly. "I was kind of wandering around wondering how to get close to the action, when I suddenly remembered that there was meant to be a turbolift around here somewhere, and thought I may as well have a look for it!"

A shudder of pain jolts Peder's body and you're reminded again that he's hurt.

"We'd better get you to a medical droid," you say. "Can you get up?"

"Sure, sure, don't fuss," he says gritting his teeth, and with a clone trooper on one side and you on the other, he slowly climbs to his feet.

"I guess you guys are on your own now," you say to the trooper leader, trying to keep the regretful tone out of your voice.

"Thanks for your help, both of you," he replies, looking from you to Peder. "It took a lot of guts and we appreciate it."

"No problem," you reply and, with one arm around Peder's shoulders, you head slowly in the direction of home.

THE END

You stand there, not moving. Godalhi clutches you tightly by the elbow.

"Did you hear me? Get inside that room! Quick, I can hear someone coming!" he yells.

"We're not going in there until we find out if that . . ." you point to the body farther down the corridor, "needs our help. If you had a medpac, we—"

"That, is dead!" replies Godalhi angrily, cutting you off. "The security system is still feeding electrical units into the corpse, which is rare I'll admit, but that's why it looks like it's moving. Nothing could've survived the system once it was tripped, I installed it myself!"

You look again and realize he's right, the movement is unnatural and jerky and you feel tears welling in your eyes.

"Come on," says Peder, grabbing your arm and pulling you toward the antechamber. "There's no time to feel sorry for it, we need to hide!"

A volley of blaster fire whistles past your head as Godalhi pushes you to the floor—you're under attack!

"You two, get behind those crates," he orders. You have no hesitation following his instructions this time!

Safe behind a huge container, Godalhi calls out to your attackers.

"I advise you to stay where you are! This whole corridor is rigged and one false movement and you're dead!"

There's silence from farther up the corridor and you wonder if your attackers have heard Godalhi, when suddenly you hear a synthetic voice call out: "Who are you?

What are you doing down here?"

"I could ask you the same question!" replies Godalhi.

There is a brief silence. "We're clone troopers with the Republican army," the voice calls back. "We landed on Teth this morning. Intelligence received indicated that the Separatists were concealing someone we were searching for on this planet. We've now found that someone and are securing the area!"

Peder looks at you, his eyes wide with astonishment.

"It didn't take them long to overpower the Separatists," he whispers.

No, it didn't, you think to yourself suspiciously, remembering the superior position the Separatists held at the top of the mesa.

You see Godalhi carefully pop his head up and assess the situation.

"I see you!" he calls, adding, "Stay where you are and I'll disarm the security system and you can tell me all about what happened."

The emphasis on the word "me" makes you think that Godalhi wants to keep your presence a secret. Maybe, like you, he's unsure whether to trust the troopers?

If you trust the clone troopers, turn to page 153.
If you think there's something weird going on, turn to page 39.

The turbolift is almost level with the open doorway when the Trandoshan gives you the go ahead and you leap toward him and he, as good as his word, grabs you and drags you into the hallway.

"I feel sick," you say, collapsing on the floor.

"I'm not sssurprised," he says bluntly. "What were you doing fooling about in a lift shaft? Hiding ssssomething?"

"Hiding something? I almost got killed!" you squeal.

Ignoring you, the Trandoshan peers down the shaft.

"I'm not lying!" you say angrily. "Who are you, anyway? What are you doing here at the monastery?"

"I could assssk the ssssame of you . . ." he begins before reading the look of annoyance on your face. "I am Quar Rohk, I have a mission that brought me here and when that mission isss complete, I shall be on my way."

"Are you working for the Separatists?" you ask.

"Working with, I possibly would accept," laughs Rohk. "But my ssssservicessss are for hire. I have no allegiance to either the Sssseparatistssss or the Republic."

An explosion rings out from somewhere close by.

"Come, we are forgetting that we're in the middle of a battle!" says Rohk, helping you to your feet. "Let uss work together, what do you sssay?"

Turn to page 75.

What are you going to do?

That split second of indecision is all Ventress needs. She grabs you and pulls you close, her eyes boring into yours.

Slowly her eyes roll back in her head and everything around you becomes hazy and indistinct like the hallway is full of smoke.

"You have chosen wisely, youngling," she says softly, as your vision begins to clear again, and before you, you see the cruel, twisted smile of your new mistress . . .

THE END

"Oh, Quar Rohk," says Ventress smoothly, coming into the room.

"I-I-I . . ." says Rohk, backing away from Ventress.

"I could have killed you straight away, but I knew you wouldn't be able to resist looking for the crystalline vertex cache and I thought it'd be much more fun to have a little sport with you first," she continues, before noticing you. "And what is this little thing? Your lunch?"

Neither of you answer. "I'm getting bored," she sighs. "So I think I'll just kill you now."

"But Ventress, you can let me go! I won't tell anyone about this cache and neither will the youngling!" he pleads, writhing in her grasp.

"That's right, you won't, because you'll be DEAD!" Ventress roars in reply, dragging Rohk out of the chamber and into the hallway. "Now prepare to die, Quar Rohk!" And from inside the chamber you hear the sound of a lightsaber igniting.

I don't want him to die like that! you think, trembling with fear. *But while Ventress is distracted, I could make an escape; it's him or me . . .*

If you help Quar Rohk, turn to page 58.
If you make a run for it, turn to page 87.

You smile to yourself, it's always been a dream of yours to see where Anakin Skywalker was brought up. And now you have the opportunity!

I think it would be okay to pay a quick visit and then go straight home, you say to yourself, as you think guiltily of what Obi-Wan would say if he knew you were taking a Credaan Spacer joyriding around the galaxy. *When am I ever going to get another chance such as this?*

Taking a deep breath, you punch in the coordinates and you're on your way!

But as you near the planet's orbit, three ships suddenly appear from behind one of Tatooine's suns and, checking the onboard computer, your worst fears are realized: MagnaGuard fighters!

If you try and out maneuver them, turn to page 182.

If you surrender, turn to page 154.

"I don't have much choice, do I?" you answer angrily. "I will become a Sith and join you in your battle against the Republic!"

"You are as brave and as clever as my servant informed me," says Dooku, pleased. "It was worth me journeying from Tatooine to see to your conversion personally."

"Yes, Master," you say easily, thrusting all thoughts from your mind.

But when you're alone, your soul is tormented by the thought that one day you will be destroyed in a battle, completely controlled by Dooku!

THE END

"My name is Janu Godalhi, I'm a friend of the Jedi Master Plo Koon. I need to approach in order to disable the security system!" he warns the clone troopers.

As Godalhi deactivates the system, you wonder at how he can have metamorphosed from peculiar old man into security expert so quickly.

It must be part of his camouflage, you think to yourself. Still keeping your heads down, you and Peder hear the sound of the security system shutting down and the clones slowly approaching.

"Thank you, sir," you hear the trooper intone. "We hadn't realized that this tunnel was so heavily protected."

You hear the trooper move off to one side and activate his comlink.

Up until this point, Janu Godalhi hasn't completely trusted the clone troopers, but now he knows that they're the real deal.

"Stop where you are!" Godalhi calls, laughing nervously and slipping back into his old man role. "I'm so sorry, I neglected to disable the field generator. That could've been nasty! I'm glad you troopers came. You saved us a wasted journey. Show yourselves!" Godalhi calls to you and Peder. "There's nothing to fear, but I'm afraid your adventure is over!"

THE END

What's going on here? What are MagnaGuards doing over Tatooine and what do they want with me?

The three fighters are on your tail. They haven't started firing, but it's probably only a matter of time . . .

Your blood runs cold at the thought of surrendering, but you have no choice; you'll never be able to outrun them in a Creedan Spacer!

Landing, you disembark to find the three MagnaGuards are waiting for you on the hot sands.

One of them gestures you to move, cutting the air with his electrostaff. "Okay!" you say, stumbling forward, your boots sinking into the sand.

When you reach the top of a high sand dune, you see a massive, round, squat tower, flanked by two narrow towers—all the same color as the surrounding desert. The Western Dune Sea!

"Is that where we're going?" you ask one of the MagnaGuards, who ignores you. "You guys shouldn't bother applying for jobs with Tatooine's Tourist Bureau," you mumble to yourself just as the MagnaGuard shoves you in the back, sending you somersaulting down the dune.

Turn to page 141.

"You said you'd follow my orders," says Godalhi, eyeing you.

"Yes, of course," you reply and, grabbing Peder, you duck into the antechamber, the approaching footsteps suddenly worrying you more than the twitching creature in the corridor.

As soon as you're through the door, you hear it clang shut behind you and a key turn in the lock.

"W-w-w-what are you doing?" you cry, with a mixture of fear and annoyance. "Why are you locking us in, Janu?"

"I'm sorry, younglings," he whispers in reply. "It's far too dangerous for you to be free while the Separatists are on Teth. I will come and free you when they have left."

"Janu, you can't leave us here! We're not children!" you call back, but there's no reply.

Peder looks at you and shrugs his shoulders.

"The man is clearly crazy, there's nothing we can do," he says resignedly, sitting on the floor, preparing himself for the long wait . . .

THE END

Your speeder bike sputters to a halt. You knew it was a risk taking the abandoned machine; after all, it must have been left behind for a reason!

The destroyer droids are nearing and, although you have three grenades left, you don't have enough to save yourself . . .

This is the end, you think resolutely, *but I'm not going down without a fight!*

"Come get me, you robotic rubbish bins!" you shout, as you lob a grenade among the first onslaught of droidekas. "A Tethan is about to take out the trash!"

THE END

By the time you've crawled carefully out of the cantina on your hands and knees, your heart is no longer pounding and you've stopped feeling like you're going to be sick!

"That was . . . amazing," Peder says, grinning broadly at you. "I thought we were deader than a krabbex!"

"Me too," you say, not quite as enthusiastically. "What kind of security expert hangs out in a cantina like that?"

"One that wants to know what type of criminal they're up against when designing a security system, I suppose," replies Peder happily. "Keep your friends close, your enemies closer, and your core market silly enough to discover their secrets!"

"Look, Peder," you begin hesitantly. "We could've been killed in there. Are you sure you want to continue looking for Janu Godalhi?"

"Absolutely!" he replies confidently. "Where shall we start?"

You let out a very deep sigh; you had a feeling he was going to ask you that . . .

Turn to page 63.

Hanging around the Senate building, making sure to exit whenever the ever-rotating guards seem to pay you too much attention, you finally catch sight of Senator Amidala, surrounded by her bodyguards, leaving the building.

Rushing toward her impetuously, you call out.

"Senator Amidala, a moment of your time please?"

Immediately two of her bodyguards swing around and face you, blasters drawn.

You stop and raise your hands and the Senator, throwing you a quick glance, is hustled forward by her remaining bodyguards.

"Don't move," growls one of them, waving his blaster menacingly. "The Senator hasn't time to talk to the likes of you."

You stare into the black hole of the blaster before you, weighing your options.

If you insist on talking to Senator Amidala, turn to page 82.

If you follow another course, turn to page 99.

Taking a deep breath, you pull off the panel cover and start randomly pushing the keypad, hoping blind luck will allow you to select the correct code, when you hear a loud click behind you, like the sound of a hundred metal crates unlocking!

Is it possible I entered the correct code? you wonder, your eyes round with amazement. Abruptly, the floor begins to shudder and in the middle of the room, you see that it's beginning to split apart and roll back, allowing you to see the chamber below.

"HAHAHAHA! The little Tethan youngling thought it had succeeded!" Ventress's voice shrieks with laughter.

She's spying on me! you think, and, as the floor draws inexorably back into the wall and the gap through which you're about to fall widens, you're suddenly no longer scared, just full of rage and the thirst for revenge.

"Only a coward would hide herself, Ventress!" you howl over the hideous clanging noise of the metal crates plummeting through the floor to the chamber below. "Is it possible that you fear me?"

You're perched on the very edge of the remaining floor, but there's nowhere to go and soon, with just the width of your boot remaining, you stumble and plunge headfirst into the room below.

Turn to page 126.

You don't have any time to lose and you quickly attempt to draw the blaster out from inside your tunic, but the weapon snags on your clothes.

In that critical time, Ventress swings around in a circle and you watch helplessly as all the troopers in the vicinity are flattened to the ground.

Letting out a little grunt of satisfaction, she turns back to you and, seeing the blaster in your trembling hand, she Force-pulls it out of your grasp and sends it flying across the courtyard.

"Would you have killed me, I wonder," she says quietly, sizing you up.

"I would have enjoyed killing you!" you yell.

"I was going to kill you, but perhaps there is a place for you after all," she replies meditatively.

"I would rather die than join you!" you spit.

"Yes, well, that can be arranged, also," she smiles. "But if you won't join me willingly, I'm sure you can be persuaded!"

Pulling you close to her, she stares unblinkingly into your eyes and the world begins to spin. "Very soon you will be under my power, youngling," Ventress murmurs. "And I will have a worthy apprentice . . ."

THE END

The battle droids, their eyes staring you down, raise their weapons to fire and, just at that instant, two things happen:

"I've got it!" you yell, pulling out your last haywire grenade and throwing it at the battle droids.

"Have no fear, youngling," says Obi-Wan at exactly the same time, Force-pushing the doors of the turbolift closed.

You both freeze as the grenade bounces off the now closed doors and lands between you.

"Open the door! Open the blasted door!" yells Kenobi, diving to pick up the grenade as you fling yourself on the control panels.

The doors immediately slide open again and Kenobi lobs the grenade among the battle droids.

"I think this is for you," he says, before Force-pushing the doors closed again.

The grenade detonates and bolts of electricity charge the air inside the turbolift, knocking you both to the ground unharmed.

"I think, if it's okay by you, you'd best leave the tricky stuff to me, hmm?" says Kenobi getting to his feet and dusting himself off.

"Oh yes, of course, Master Kenobi!" you breathe, awestruck by your proximity to the legend.

"Yes, well . . ." he says, eyeing you doubtfully. "Seems you have the advantage of knowing who I am. And you are?"

"I'm from Teth, General," you say proudly. "My friend and I saw your gunships arrive and—"

Obi-Wan Kenobi raises his hand, palm out, to halt you

mid-sentence.

"Yes, I think I can guess the rest. I've had quite a lot of experience with inquisitive younglings in my time, and one in particular," he smiles to himself.

He must mean Anakin Skywalker! you think, excited and flattered to be compared to your hero.

"Now, youngling, I think it's time for you to go home and for me to return to my ship. Our mission here at Hutt Castle has been a great success," says Kenobi, clapping his hands together and clasping them to his chest.

"B-B-But, General, the Separatists have overrun the monastery, surely you can't leave now?" you say.

The doors slide open onto an empty passageway and Kenobi ducks his head out to ensure the coast is clear, before exiting the turbolift.

"Don't worry," he calls reassuringly over his shoulder, as he strides up the passageway. "Now that the Separatists have lost their prize, they'll leave your planet to pursue an alternative course of action."

"But, Master Kenobi," you call, trotting to keep up. "What about the plans I saw?"

"The plans?" asks Kenobi, stopping dead and turning slowly to face you. "What plans are these?"

Turn to page 26.

Where there were once walls, there is nothing but rubble, the explosion obliterating everything in its path.

"We were lucky we weren't killed," you say, limping beside Kenobi.

"Luck had nothing to do with it, youngling," he replies. "That explosion is nothing compared to the strength of the Force! "

"But what about the crystalline vertex and the plans for the superweapon?" you ask. "What are we going to do about that?"

"Gone . . . all gone. Look around, could mere minerals have survived this catastrophe?" replies Kenobi. "Although I have no doubt that the Separatists have archives of their plans, it will take time to amass such quantities of crystalline vertex again to pay for it. That's all thanks to you, youngling!"

"Obi-Wan, come in?" asks a disembodied voice from Kenobi's comlink.

"Kenobi, here. Anakin, have you reached Tatooine yet?"

"Almost, but we ran into old—" begins Skywalker, before being cut off.

"Anakin, did you get shot down again?" Obi-Wan's voice is stern, but you see his eyes shining with mirth.

"Yes!" someone new yells in the background.

"I'm still cleaning up your other mess, but I'll get there as soon as I can," Kenobi adds, smiling, but there is no reply.

"Anakin?" says Kenobi. "Blast. He's out of range." He turns to you.

"I must take a transport back to the *Spirit of the Republic*, as my fighter was badly damaged when I arrived on Teth. Perhaps you'd like to accompany me to the rendezvous point?"

"Yes please, Master Kenobi!" you say excitedly.

Turn to page 8.

You're awoken by a gentle tap at the door.

"I hope you're well rested, youngling," says Kenobi as he enters the pod. "I didn't want to wake you, but the *Spirit of the Republic* is on course to meet Anakin Skywalker and I need to know without delay what decision you have come to regarding your future."

Sitting up and rubbing the sleep from your eyes, you grin happily at Obi-Wan.

"Master Kenobi," you say. "While I was sleeping, I dreamed of what happened at the monastery and of Ventress, but I felt no fear. Instead, I felt exhilarated and strong."

"That is an encouraging sign, youngling," replies Kenobi.

"What I'm trying to say, Master," you say shyly, "is that I wish to join the Jedi and attend the Academy. If you'll still have me, of course!"

Obi-Wan Kenobi laughs and slaps you on the back, nodding his head in assent.

"It would be best if we could return immediately to Coruscant so you may take your place at the Academy, but as I've mentioned, we are needed on Tatooine to support Anakin in his mission. So you will accompany us," says Kenobi, a huge grin spreading across his face. "And for Pidarts' sake, try to stay out of trouble this time, yes?"

THE END

You dive after Peder as you hear the crackle of laser fire pass over your head! Peder hauls you to your feet and you both sprint away, running until you collapse under the camouflaging leaves of a giant randoos bush.

"Gransk! I thought we were done for," says Peder.

"Me too!" you say, thinking of the droid and its winking, red eye . . .

You sit in silence for a moment before Peder says, "I wonder what's happening at the B'omarr monk monastery."

"Well, isn't it obvious? The Separatists must be using it as a secret base or something," you reply.

"That's what you think? There must be something more to it than tha—" Peder suddenly stops mid-sentence. "You know who would know, don't you?"

You're afraid to ask. After all, Peder's last bright idea almost got you killed.

"Janu Godalhi!" says Peder, not waiting for your guess.

The legendary historian, security expert, and ex-constable of Teth.

"Janu Godalhi? Why should he bother to talk to us?" you ask.

"Because," says Peder, getting to his feet, "he owes my dad money. Now, come on, we're going to Raidos."

Turn to page 173.

The AT-TE shudders as it bends its hard carapace and places its front two legs on the side of the cliff. The middle two legs follow, one of which you're gripping on to like your life depends on it. And finally the last two attach themselves as you move your position to reflect the change from the horizontal to the vertical.

As it marches steadily upward, you remember that there is quite a considerable overhang near the top of the mesa, and you realize that your already precarious position straddling the leg will become even more hazardous.

I have to get up front, near the projectile cannon, you think to yourself, figuring the more surface area to hold on to, the more secure you will be.

Then you make the fatal mistake of looking down!

From the vantage point of this height, you can easily see scorch marks and bits of wreckage from at least one flaming AT-TE that has plummeted to the jungle floor. Surrounding the debris, you glimpse the broken bodies of the clone troopers that fell, or were shot, while trying to scale the cliff.

You take a deep breath and slowly pull yourself along the seesawing leg until you reach the primary drive motor, and drag yourself hand over hand around it until you can wedge your feet safely on the body of the AT-TE.

"So far, so good," you say, your voice sounding alien and muffled inside the trooper helmet. "Only thirty feet or so to go . . ."

You know you'll have to climb up the side of the AT-TE

to avoid being spotted by the gunner positioned directly behind the projectile cannon.

Although what's he going to do if he sees you, wave hello?

You smile briefly to yourself, as you stretch out your arms and, using your fingers to find gaps in the armor plating, you heave yourself along the shuddering body.

Sweat is pouring down your face and you close your eyes and scale the body by touch alone.

After what seems like a lifetime, you reach the front of the AT-TE and, being careful to avoid both the range finder and antipersonnel laser cannons, you heave yourself into a position of relative safety.

I made it! you think to yourself, tears of relief springing to your eyes.

It's only then, looking up at the overhang, that it occurs to you how exposed you're going to be when the AT-TE reaches the lip of the cliff in a few short minutes' time.

No weapon, no body armor, no plan! Can things get any worse?

Turn to page 20.

KA-BOOM!

The force of the explosion knocks you to the ground and you look up to see the destroyer droid disintegrate in a huge fireball!

The clone troopers have seen that you're in trouble and have created a diversion. "Over here, you Separatist nightmare!" you hear one yell.

You take the opportunity to race to the doorway and hear the woman screeching behind you as she battles the troopers. Flying through the door, you hide behind a column in the back of the room.

All of a sudden, you hear a squadron of clone troopers come in the door, pursued by the super battle droids. Laser fire ricochets off the column and, drawing your blaster, you fire on the Separatist machines!

But the super battle droids keep coming. Filing through the doorway, they're joined by more destroyer droids, and the clone troopers begin to succumb to the overwhelming numbers of the Separatist Army.

You see the woman from the quadrangle, her dual lightsabers deflecting lasers and you realize it's hopeless; the troopers can't hold back the inevitable. You have to run, before the droids see you.

Darting out from behind the column, you sprint for the stairs. Down you run; you don't stop until you can barely hear the noise above you, only then collapsing on the ground, gasping for breath.

You notice a computer screen flickering across the way,

the image stuck in an endless loop. You go over to examine the screen more closely.

On the display, a schematic of a planet or moon slowly revolves, before zooming into close up. You see it has components like air filtration, flight decks and eight tributary lasers shooting out to form one super-laser. It's a weapon! A huge, planet-sized weapon!

Before you have time to see more, static fills the screen and readings from a holo-log flash up, detailing deliveries of enormous quantities of crystalline vertex, one of the most precious commodities in the galaxy, being made at the B'omarr monk monastery!

You've heard rumors that the monastery has been, or is being, used by smugglers, but what if the Separatists were using it, too? What if the Separatists were amassing a cache of crystalline vertex in order to finance a superweapon capable of destroying the Republic Army?

The display sizzles and the image of the superweapon flashes back on-screen and the loop starts again.

You hear the clone troopers heading down to your level.

Racing to the bottom of the stairs and looking up, you make out a flash of lasers as they descend the stairs to the floor above yours.

For a second, you're frozen with indecision, but then you notice a shadow. Running over, you discover a beat-up speeder bike.

The spluttering comlink sends sparks showering. If you don't attempt to find out who's behind the superweapon now, by the time you find another terminal, the main comlink could be damaged. But the droids are closing in . . .

If you hack the computer, click on box K on-screen and type code word HACK, or turn to page 104.

If you need help and take the speeder bike, click on box E on-screen and type SPEEDERBIKE, or turn to page 14.

If you hide in the hope that the impending danger will pass, turn to page 7.

You know what Godalhi says is true, it is dangerous, but you can't just let the poor injured creature lie there suffering!

"You don't understand," you hear Godalhi call far behind you. "The security system! It's shooting electricity into the body, that's why it's moving! The security system is still activ . . ."

ZAAAAAAAAAAAAAAAAP!!

THE END

Racing your speeder bikes, you soon reach the main gates of Raidos. As you pull up to speak to a couple of Barabel sentries on guard duty, you can already smell the corruption in the stale air that hangs over the most dangerous and lawless city on Teth.

"And whatsssss do we have here?" asks the slimy guard.

"Very good quesssssssssstion," says his mate, flicking his scaly tail and eyeing the speeder bikes meditatively. Before you can stop him, Peder pipes up.

"We're looking for Janu Godalhi," he says. "Do you know where we can find him?"

"Janu Godalhi, you sssssssssssay? Hmmmm, maybe we doesssss and maybe we don'tssssss," replies one of the guards cryptically.

You've been expecting this. "What will it take to jog your memory?" you ask, knowing full well you have very little money to grease the cold, scaly palms of these two specimens.

"A ssssspeeder bike might do the tricksssssssssssssssss," replies the sentry as innocently as a seven-foot-tall reptilian life form, with a set of teeth to rival a Graculan can!

If you hand over a speeder bike, turn to page 29.
If you refuse to part with a speeder bike, turn to page 128.

It's too dangerous! If the security droid sees you, it's just as likely to fire on you as the mine owner, but it's a gamble. What if there isn't another opportunity?

You lay still and after a few more questions from the droid, the transport lurches forward and you are thrown hard against the back of the seat.

"Watch it back there," the mine owner growls. "Don't you try any funny business."

Battered and bruised, you lie as still as you can when you suddenly feel a strange sensation, like the planet is dropping out from under you!

We're in a turbolift!

Next thing you hear is an elevator droid's voice chiming: "Level 324—Gas Refinery and Miner's Quarters."

And you've reached your destination . . . welcome to a life of slavery!

THE END

You drop to your knees, the blaster falling from your hand sending it clattering across the floor.

"I had to do it!" you scream. "I had to!"

"Yeah, you did have to," replies Quar Rohk unconcerned. "And I'm going to have to get rid of you now."

You look up at him, tears running down your face.

"What? You said it was him or me!" you say, the confusion showing plainly on your face.

"What I should have said was it'ssss you and him," he replies, aiming the blaster at you. "I can't let you go, you'll tell Jabba the Hutt that I ssstole his treasure off the Sssseparatissstsss."

"Why? Why are you doing this to me?" you exclaim.

"Jusssst the Trandoshan in me I guessssssssssssss," Quar Rohk replies.

THE END

"Can you please tell the benevolent Jabba that I apologize for my display of bad manners," you say, bowing to Jabba, who nods in acknowledgment. "And that of course I will tell him anything he wants to know about the cache of crystalline vertex."

Pleased that you're being so cooperative, Jabba demands to know where the cache is hidden, who owns it and a million other things. You invent plausible answers to all his questions, stressing that you know exactly where the cache can be found within the warren of chambers and hallways that make up the B'omarr monk monastery.

"It's quite useless to think you'll find the crystalline vertex by merely wandering randomly around the place," you say shrewdly.

Finally, out of questions, Jabba silently watches you, clearly making up his mind whether to trust you or not.

"Sloopu maka trewara. Pero fundoo slakee patoo Tatooine!" he says at last.

"The majestic Jabba wishes you to know that, for the moment, you are more useful to him alive than dead," says TC-70, and you breathe a sigh of relief.

"But," she continues, "If you are found to be lying to him, you are going to regret you ever came to Tatooine."

Don't worry, you think fatalistically. *I already do!*

THE END

"We need to find the cantina Janu Godalhi drinks in, I suppose," you reply doubtfully.

"Well, that shouldn't be too difficult," says Peder sarcastically, throwing up his hands in utter disgust. "There must be a zillion cantinas in Raidos!"

"And we'll check them all one at a time," you say patiently, pushing your way into the heaving mass of bodies, reptilian, avian, and mammalian alike.

You haven't gone very far when you see three merry Bothans, arm in arm, come reeling out of a cantina and into the street.

"In here," you say to Peder, as you pull across the dusty curtain and enter the surprisingly airy interior of the cantina.

Swiftly, any confidence you've been feeling disappears as you note how many eyes, ears, and tentacles are sizing you up.

"I don't feel very good about leaving the speeder bike outsi . . . oh . . ." says Peder, coming in the door behind you and feeling sixty pairs of eyes on him.

"It will be quite fine, young Master," says an oily voice at Peder's side.

You turn to face a foul-smelling Devaronian, who smiles at you.

"Now, what refreshments can I bring you, younglings?"

"Oh, we'll just have . . . whatever," you say, gesturing broadly and mentally counting the credits in your tunic pocket.

"Take a seat," the Devaronian says, his horns glinting in the light.

You find a spare table near the door where a gap in the door-curtain allows you to keep half an eye on the speeder bike.

"I have a bad feeling about this," you say to Peder, who nods his head in agreement. But before he has time to reply, an unwanted guest has invaded your table.

"Hello, younglings," grunts the Trandoshan male as he slips into the seat opposite you. "I couldn't help but notice that you ssseem a little . . . lossst. You are . . . looking for sssomeone perhapsss? Or it's just advice you need?"

"Ahhhhhem!" From over the Trandoshan's shoulder you hear someone pointedly clearing his throat.

The Trandoshan quickly spins around in his chair, and spies the towering Miraluka standing behind him.

"What do you want?" he snarls at the new arrival.

"What do I want? I want to warn these younglings against you!" it spits back at him, before turning to you. "Don't trust this . . . this . . . this . . . creature!"

Very soon, the two of them are ignoring you and arguing heatedly between themselves about which of them you and Peder should trust!

"While these two are distracted, I'll ask the cantina owner if he knows where Godalhi is today," whispers Peder, rolling his eyes.

If you trust the Miraluka and believe it is trying to save you from an unscrupulous Trandoshan, turn to page 73.

If you leave the cantina, turn to page 13.

If you let Peder talk to the cantina owner and let the Trandoshan and the Miraluka battle it out, click on box C on-screen and type code word LET, or turn to page 114.

You stare at the timer . . . 5, 4, 3 . . .

Then, blaster in hand, you fling yourself into the hall-way and dash back to Obi-Wan Kenobi, just as the bombs go off!

CRRRRRR-BOOOM! BOOM-BAM-KA-BOOOOOM! TSS-KKK-BOOM!

The force of the blast throws you both to the floor, as a gigantic fireball rips up the hallway and through the battle droids, their systems malfunctioning in its terrifying heat.

Flames lick the stone walls and ceiling and, in no time at all, the entire length of the hallway is ablaze, as bits of stone rain down on you and dust fills your nose and mouth.

"Quick!" says Kenobi, dragging you to your feet. "We have to get out of here, this whole wing is about to collapse!"

Picking your way quickly through the rubble, you wonder whether Ventress has made it out alive . . .

Turn to page 163.

You pull the Credaan Spacer's starmap up on-screen and study all the places you could possibly visit in the galaxy . . . but none of them look as inviting as Teth.

Maybe I've had enough adventure for a while, you think to yourself, before remembering that there's still this Janu Godalhi person to meet and who knows what being his assistant will entail.

If he's a friend of Obi-Wan Kenobi's, you think amused, *there'll probably be plenty more chances of getting shot at, blown up, and generally threatened!*

And setting the coordinates, you engage the ship and head for home.

THE END

I wonder what this hunk of junk can do? you ask yourself, doubtfully looking around the cockpit of the outdated Credaan Spacer with the MagnaGuard fighters still on your tail.

I've got to try to lose these guys, because I don't think they're the type that take prisoners!

All three fighters are spaced out in formation behind you and, checking your onboard computer, you realize they're either trying to force you to land, or about to use you for target practice.

"Engage reverse thrusters!" you yell at the onboard system. "Full power to rear defense shields!"

Suddenly, the spacer shoots backward into the space created by the fighters, and you're flying in reverse before dropping vertically and heading to the surface of Tatooine.

In a moment, all three MagnaGuard fighters have changed course, too, and pursue you closely, letting off a volley of cannon fire.

This is going to be a close shave! you think, the hot desert of Tatooine rushing up to meet you. But when you're as close as you dare, you pull the spacer out of its dive and swoop up again, only feet away from plummeting into the planet's surface.

This maneuver proves too much for one MagnaGuard fighter and it collides nose-first into the desert, kicking sand high up into the air.

One down, two to go . . .

You climb quickly, the two remaining fighters following

close behind, buffeting your ship with their relentless attack.

"Rear defense shields at 30 percent." Oh, for Pandit's sake!

"All power to forward defense shields," you order loudly and, turning the spacer 180 degrees, you mount a frontal attack on the two remaining fighters.

And now the pursued becomes the pursuer!

"Forward defense shields at 25 percent," says the onboard computer.

"You could have told me that before!" you yell, and now nose to nose, the MagnaGuard fighters head straight for you.

"Forward defense shields at 15 percent."

Let's see who'll pull out first, you think grimly to yourself, remembering how you and Peder would play "feng'aa chicken" on your speeder bikes.

You hold your nerve then . . . if they pull out to the right, then you go left . . .

But you hadn't counted on their training and suddenly a new, harsh voice spits viciously over the spacer's commport.

"We will never yield, prepare to DIE!" shrieks the MagnaGuard.

"Forward defense shields at 5 percent," drones the computer.

In that case, no one is yielding! you think furiously. *If I hold my nerve and use this spacer as a giant flying bomb . . . then these two particular MagnaGuards won't be bothering anyone else again . . .*

THE END

"But before we do anything," he says, laughing at the look of astonishment on your face, "we'd better get out of here first!"

The turbolift doors slide open and you're back where you started, the enormous main doors of the monastery in front of you, framing a Republic starfighter.

"Ah, my ship," says Obi-Wan, striding forward. "Right where I left it."

The hallways and chambers are deserted and as you look around you're saddened by the thought of this beautiful structure being completely demolished.

"Wait, Master Kenobi!" you say, chasing after him. "You're going to completely destroy the B'omarr monk monastery? But how? Why?"

"While our clone troopers evacuate, I'll order explosive experts to lay charges around the hallways. I don't have time to hunt out a treasure trove and it's too dangerous to leave those levels of crystalline vertex just lying around where anyone could get them. My mission is yet to be completed and I must leave Teth immediately. Anything else you want to know?" he asks, half amused by your questions.

"Yes," you say boldly. "Can I come with you? Can I train to be a Jedi?"

Now it's Obi-Wan's turn to look dumbfounded!

"You have certainly shown yourself to be useful, youngling," he says doubtfully. "But there's much more to being a Jedi than you think. There are other ways you can aid the Republic fight against the Separatists."

"Please, Master Kenobi," you blurt out. "I won't disappoint you!"

"I will let you accompany me back to the *Spirit of the Republic*," says Obi-Wan seriously. "But once there, I want you to think very carefully about your future, youngling. Your impetuous nature may have you desiring things that you will later regret ever wishing for."

You squeeze into the back of his ship without replying, even though he's absolutely right; you do make decisions that you come to regret . . .

As he engages the starfighter, Kenobi contacts his captains and briefly explains what he knows of the super-weapon and the crystalline vertex cache, giving orders to demolish the monastery once the last clone trooper has been evacuated.

Before the ship has left Teth's orbit en route to the Jedi Cruiser, you fall into an exhausted sleep. Your dreams are full of whirling images of droidekas, a crystalline vertex, and Ventress. You only stir when you feel yourself lifted out of the back of the ship and placed in a sleeping pod.

"Now don't think anymore about making a decision tonight, youngling," you hear Obi-Wan say. "There'll be time enough for that when you awaken."

"The answer came to me in a dream," you mumble, struggling to open your eyes. "I've already made up my mind . . ."

And that's the last thing you remember before falling back asleep.

If you follow the way of the Jedi, turn to page 165.
If you help the Republic in your own way, turn to page 27.

"I-I-I feel strange," you say again, rubbing your eyes and looking up at Plo Koon. "The base is just about to be attacked and I feel kind of . . . peaceful, isn't that strange?"

"It's not so strange," replies Plo Koon, his hand passing over your face again. "It's too dangerous for you here . . ."

"Yes . . . perhaps it's not so strange," you mumble, your head feeling full of cotton wool. "It's too dangerous for me here."

"If you're feeling unwell, it might be a good idea to leave here immediately," he says quietly, repeating his movements. "Hurry home right away, give up any thoughts of going to the monastery."

"Yes, I'll go home right away," you murmur as you turn around and leave the base. "I'll give up all thoughts of going to the monastery . . ."

THE END

"I-I-I'll join the dark side," you whisper, hardly believing what you're saying.

And looking up into Ventress's face, you don't see the exultant expression you would have expected from a ruthless dark acolyte, but you see the pitying look of a creature that knows what the decision may cost you . . .

THE END

The spaceport is nearby and as you and Pwi'lin enter, you immediately see the *Rindoon Dart*, her engines roaring in preparation for her departure.

"Oh, she's beautiful!" you exclaim.

"Isn't she!" says Pwi'lin, gratified by your interest. "Come and have a look at her twin blasters, and then I really must go!"

Ducking under a wing, you see Pwi'lin's first mate sitting in the copilot's seat. He gestures to Pwi'lin, pointing at his wrist, the galaxy-wide sign for "Hurry Up"!

"I'm coming, I'm coming!" bellows Pwi'lin over the howl of the engines, before pointing out a newly installed laser cannon.

"You can see that the new position of the hyperspace drive enhances its capabilities," he says conversationally, as you lean in for a closer look.

Suddenly, he grabs you tightly and hustles you up the entry ramp.

"Hey! What are you doing, Pwi'lin?" you ask, confused.

"You're coming with us!" replies Pwi'lin, tightening his grip and pulling you farther inside the *Rindoon Dart* as the entry ramp closes.

"Go!" yells Pwi'lin to his first mate, who engages the engines and you fly out of the spaceport.

"W-w-what are you doing? Where are you taking me?" you cry.

Pwi'lin picks up a pair of security bracelets and fastens

one armlet around your wrist and the other to a bench that runs along the walls of the hold.

"We're going to Cloud City," he says matter-of-factly, grabbing a second pair of bracelets and securing your feet to the bottom of the bench. "And when we get there, I'm selling you to a mine owner I know."

"What?" you say, appalled. "You're . . . you're a slave trader?"

"Yes, I am," replies Pwi'lin, stuffing a gag in your mouth. "Now shut your hole, you're giving me a headache!"

When the *Rindoon Dart* lands in Cloud City, there's an unscrupulous mine owner waiting for you. Still gagged and cuffed, you're shoved into the back of a transport, a dirty tarpaulin pulled up over you.

What am I going to do! If I try and signal for help, who's to say that anyone's going to believe I've been kidnapped? I'm sure the mine owner is capable of telling any number of lies to disprove my story, you think bitterly, tears springing to your eyes. *He's probably had a lot of practice!*

You feel the transport begin to slow down and come to a halt.

We're here! Wherever "here" is, you think sadly, giving up any thoughts of rescue, when suddenly you hear voices.

"Do you have your authorization papers?" a security droid intones.

"Yes, I have them right here," you hear the mine owner reply.

A security checkpoint! Will you take a chance and try to escape?

If you think it's worth running the risk of being disbelieved, or worse, turn to page 23.

If you wait for a better opportunity, turn to page 174.

"You promised you'd do as I asked!" hisses Godalhi angrily.

"I know I did, but if you . . ." you start to say, before realizing that you're wasting your time reasoning with Godalhi and you dart off down the corridor toward the injured being.

"You must come back. It's too dangerous for you!" you hear him call after you desperately.

There's something in his tone that makes you reconsider your options . . .

If you heed his warning, turn to page 116.
If you ignore him, turn to page 172.